D1240383

THROWING HEARTS

N.R. WALKER

COPYRIGHT

Cover Art: N.R. Walker and SJ York
Editor: Boho Edits
Publisher: BlueHeart Press
Throwing Hearts © 2020 N.R. Walker

All Rights Reserved:

Warning

Trademarks:

BLURB

A fun and sexy romance where the kiln isn't the only thing that's scorching hot.

Leo Secombe loves his life, and he's convinced himself he's happy to be single. In his spare time, he keeps himself busy at a local LGBTQ centre that pairs a younger person with a community elder to help them feel included in today's rainbow family. Leo and Clyde have been buddies for a few years now, and signing up for a pottery class seems like fun.

Merrick Bowman has been so focused on getting his pottery business up and running that he's forgotten how to date. How to live, even. But when a young, bubbly Leo and an older, grumpy Clyde walk through his door, Merrick has no idea how much Leo is about to centre his world.

Throwing clay has been Merrick's entire life, but Leo's about to change all that. Maybe Merrick's ready to throw caution to the wind. And maybe he's ready to finally throw his heart on the line.

Throwing Hearts is 55,000-words.

THROWING
Hearts

N.R. WALKER

CHAPTER ONE

LEO SECOMBE

I KNOCKED on the front door, a little louder than I normally would have so he would hear. "Clyde? It's me, Leo."

I heard a door close inside the flat, followed by a familiar grumbling. "Yeah, yeah. Hold your horses." The peephole darkened as he peered through it, and I smiled for him. A moment later, the rattling of chains and locks took a few long seconds before the door opened inward. Clyde was short and stout, with grey hair and heavy eyebrows, and he wore tan pants and a blue T-shirt tucked in. He also wore a permanent scowl. When I first met him, he reminded me of Sam the Eagle, the angry blue Muppet bird, and the more I got to know him, the more he reminded me of him.

"Come in, come in," he said, shuffling back with his walking stick. He clearly got a better look at my shirt. "Jiminy Cricket, Leo. Is that what the gays are wearing these days?"

I looked down at my Hawaiian-style shirt. It was black with pale pink flowers, and along with my black shorts and black Vans, it was a pretty cool outfit. I gave him a nod.

"Yep. All the gays. It's our uniform now, Clyde. I was going to order one in your size."

He rolled his eyes and smiled. "Shut the door, will you? Suppose you'll want a cup of tea."

"That'd be great, thanks." I closed the door and followed Clyde into his kitchen. It was a small studio flat built in the Art Deco era, and given it was part of an aged-care living complex, it never got an upgrade. His tiny kitchen had old lino flooring and fake wooden laminate cupboards; his kitchen bench was fake marble Laminex. His carpets were old and worn, his bathroom small and dated. Everything was either brown or beige. But it was all clean and tidy and perfect for him.

He was seventy-one now; he lived alone and had done for a long time. Actually, he'd lived alone longer than my twenty-eight years. He was kind of grumpy, but that was all part of his charm.

He set about making two cups of tea, boiling water in the jug and putting the teabags in the cups. There were no fancy brands or trendy blends of tea with Clyde. Not that I minded. He was on a pension, and honestly, I appreciated everything he offered.

See, Clyde grumbled about most things, but I knew he appreciated my visits and our outings. I'd first met Clyde two years ago as part of the Bridge-the-Gap program at Arcus, my local LGBTQIA+ centre in New Farm, Brisbane. The aim of the Bridge-the-Gap program was to ease the isolation and loneliness of our LGBT seniors and pair them with a younger person for social outings and companionship.

I'd been chatting with a barista at my local café, who just happened to be cute and really friendly, and when he suggested I check out the local rainbow centre, I heartily agreed. Okay, so I agreed because I was hopeful of running into Hottie McCoffee, but as it turned out, the centre was great and Hottie McCoffee already had a boyfriend.

Over the next few months on my days off, I ended up helping out with a few things at the centre and we'd run a few days for our senior gays. And, long story short, the Bridge-the-Gap program was born, and when a group of us had a movie outing, I met Clyde.

Every Friday and every second spare day for the last two years, we'd team up and do something. It wasn't always exciting. Sometimes we'd go into Arcus and chill, or I'd just come over to his place with a packet of his favourite short-breads and we'd chat and drink tea for hours. Sometimes we'd play cards, or I'd help him with his groceries. Sometimes we did movies. Sometimes I'd take him to drag shows, which he loved.

But this visit was the beginning of something new, and I was really looking forward to it. Actually, when the program director suggested it, I jumped at the idea. Clyde wasn't too excited . . .

"Suppose I can't talk you out of going," he said.

I sipped my tea. "Nope. And you're excited to go, don't lie to me."

He grumbled something I couldn't quite decipher, but the more he grumbled, the more I smiled. It was why we were so compatible. He glared at me but eventually huffed, resigned. "Who else is going to be there?"

"Uh, Shirley and Joan, and Harvey. I think Peter was a yes, but he had his hip done two weeks ago, remember?"

He sighed and rolled his eyes. His bushy grey eyebrows stuck out in all directions with wild hairs. "Oh, that reminds me. Need me to book an appointment at Joe's for you?" I motioned to his hair but I knew Joe the barber would attack those unruly eyebrows. No self-respecting gay man would let another gay man out of his shop with those still intact.

"No," he barked. "He cut my hair too short and charged me fifteen dollars."

Pretty sure Joe charged everyone else fifty, but whatever. Clyde grumbled about a lot of things, but the price of stuff was usually the most he grumbled about. Prices, politics, and supermarket bread were his usual targets, but I was used to him. Why supermarket bread? He'd been a baker for fifty-something years and, as he told me often, he was appalled by what we called bread today. "Well, go and get your shoes on or we'll be late," I ordered. "We can't be late on our first day."

"Four weeks of this rot," he blustered, then drained his teacup and sat it in the sink. "Whose idea was this?"

"Well, you could have chosen swimming?"

He snorted as he shuffled out to put his shoes on. "My days are numbered, son. I've made it this far without seeing Frank Crossman in his swimming togs. Don't want to chance it now."

I tried not to laugh. "Leave Frank alone. He's a nice guy. Just because he's sweet on you . . ."

"Frank's sweet on no one but himself." Clyde groaned as he stood up, shoes on, and grumbled a bit at his knee for not properly kneeing. "And Marcie Yang was doing the knitting club one. If I had to listen to her prattle on for any longer than necessary, I'd take one of Rona's crochet needles and stuff it in my ear."

I laughed and handed him his walking stick. "Come on. This is gonna be great fun."

He snatched his stick and grumbled some more as he shuffled to the door. "Whereabouts is this place again?"

"Just in Newstead. Ten minutes away." Well, five

minutes to drive there, but five minutes for Clyde to walk the fifty metres to my car.

He shook his head as he opened his front door. "Can't believe I let you talk me into this."

"Aw, come on, Clyde," I said, grinning at him as I walked past. I waited in the hall for him to pull his door closed. "Pottery class sounds awesome!"

"Well, just so you know, I'm doing this for you." He waited for me to open the foyer door for him, which I did.

I laughed because, yeah, while this whole arrangement was for him, we both knew I enjoyed it as much as he did. "Of course you are."

He grumbled as he shuffled past me, out into the sunny Brisbane morning. A few kilometres' drive and a handful of minutes later, we found a parking spot outside the ceramics studio in Newstead. It was called Kil'n Time and that alone made me smile. But it was a trendy store. It obviously used to be an old warehouse—many of the stores here were—with white walls inside and exposed black piping made to look cool. There were tall, old-fashioned windows spanning the fifteen-foot ceilings, and I could smell coffee before we'd even gone inside.

"Oh, all right, all right," Clyde groused as he opened his car door. "Anything that makes you smile like that can't be too bad." I laughed and waited for him to get to the door to the ceramics studio before holding it open for him and following him inside.

CHAPTER TWO

MERRICK BOWMAN

"HOW MANY ARE WE EXPECTING?" Ciara asked. She was the barista in the small café that was at the front of my ceramics studio, and given the amount of time we both spent there, we'd become good friends. Well, the coffee shop was more of a point of sale for our ceramicware, but it was always busy.

"There's eight booked in," I replied, looking over my bookings sheet. It was a great concept, and when I was first approached by Arcus, the local LGBTQ+ centre, about the idea of running discount classes for older LGBT folk, I'd happily agreed. "It should be fun."

"Sounds it," Ciara said as she restocked the milk fridge. "I love the idea of getting the oldies out and about and trying new things."

"Me too," I replied, giving her a smile. My thoughts went to my Uncle Donny, though I dismissed any likelihood of him joining such a thing.

The phone rang and I left the café and walked through the studio to answer it. By the time I'd finished answering questions about mid-week classes, my Friday morning class had arrived. With my clipboard in hand, I walked over to them, just as the last two gentlemen walked in.

"Nice of you to show up, Clyde," one older woman said to the two men last to arrive. She looked at her watch and pursed her lips in a smile.

"Ah, Shirley," the man I deduced was Clyde replied flatly. "I see your plastic surgeon couldn't do anything about your mouth."

I stopped, my welcome stuck in my throat. *Did he really just . . . ?*

The younger woman with Shirley rolled her eyes. "Would you two stop it?"

The younger guy with Clyde laughed, but he pulled out a seat for him. "Take a seat, and be nice," he said to Clyde. He gave the others a nod, then he looked at me. "Sorry about that."

I'd be lying if I said the guy with Clyde wasn't cute. He had short blond hair, a bit of stubble, and he was wearing a black floral shirt. He had an unconventional handsomeness. His eyes were a striking blue, but his smile . . .

Wow.

It was one of those honest and natural smiles, the kind that seemed rare these days. Not completely symmetrical, but carefree and utterly mesmerising.

If a smile could be *wabi-sabi*, he had it.

Beautifully imperfect.

Realising I'd probably been staring, and definitely hadn't spoken, I cleared my throat and focused. "Good morning," I began. "My name is Merrick, and I'm the owner here at Kil'n Time. Thank you for being here! I'm actually really excited to get started with you guys today. We have four lessons together, but first we just need to run through some basics."

I showed them the essentials. The main studio held a long table with eight seats either side, which was where they were seated. There was a storeroom, a clean-up station, and a room off behind the café that had the pottery wheels, not that these guys would be using those just yet. I pointed out the bathrooms and ran through some mandatory OH&S and safety-first stuff and finally had them move up the long table to sit at the end with the most natural light.

Once they were comfortable, I put a smallish lump of clay in front of each of them. "We're going to start by making some pinch pots," I explained. "It's easy and fun, and something you can use." They all eyed the clay. One lady poked hers, but the cute guy picked his up, and feeling the weight of it in his hand, he grinned.

That wabi-sabi smile caught my eye, but then he leaned in and nudged Clyde, making the older man chuckle. They clearly had a good friendship, and I was intrigued by him.

Without knowing him at all, he was obviously the kind of guy who took time to improve the life of someone else. The kind of guy who made the effort to bring an older gent into a pottery-beginners class, in a bid to help him reconnect with the gay community. The kind of guy who had a smile that could uncentre me.

Then he threw his head back and laughed at something Clyde said. His laughter was light and contagious, the kind that made other people laugh. And that was it. Like something profound had just walked into my studio, like something tugged at a long-forgotten heartstring . . .

I had to know more.

"Let's start with names," I said, glancing at my clipboard

and booking sheet. I had a short list of names, and who was buddied up with who, and considering he was partnered with Clyde, I was guessing that made him Leo. I looked right at him and smiled. "And you are?"

CHAPTER THREE

LEO

I WASN'T EXPECTING the pottery guy to be a hottie. Well, I had no clue what to expect, but a young, hot, gay teacher hadn't factored on my day's agenda.

He hadn't introduced himself as gay or announced it in any way, but my gaydar pinged. Actually, that wasn't all that pinged. And the way he looked right at me when he asked us to introduce ourselves . . . I felt like a butterfly pinned to a board. Okay, so that might be a little dramatic. But I felt *something*. A rush, or a thrill, as he pinned me with his eyes. What did he ask me? Oh yeah. My name. "I'm Leo Secombe."

Merrick had short blackish hair, or really dark brown, depending on how the light caught it. His eyes, which stood out against his pale skin, were just as dark as his hair, and he had scruff along his jaw. He wore a blue business shirt, sleeves rolled to his elbows, with navy workman's trousers and brown work boots. It was an odd ensemble, but it somehow worked.

He went around the eight of us—four oldies and four

young'uns, as Clyde called us—and after introductions were made and aprons put on, he turned our attention to the clay. "We need to wedge it into a ball shape," he said, then picked up Harvey's piece and did this roll-knead manoeuvre. "Like this. We need to be firm but gentle, with a slow but constant pressure to push any air bubbles out. See? Not too firm, not too gentle."

I snorted. "That's what he said," I murmured. Clyde coughed to cover his laugh, though I think my smile gave us away.

Merrick glanced our way with a hint of humour in his eyes. "Be careful not to fold and create air pockets. Just pushing and turning, pushing and turning. Air pockets tend to make clay explode in the kiln, and if we could not do that, that'd be great."

He watched and helped a few of us who weren't too sure. He made it look so easy, but I wasn't convinced I was doing it right. Then I looked over at Clyde . . . He was a pro! Like he'd done it a thousand times before. "How are you . . . ?"

"Oh, Clyde, that's really good," Merrick said, seeing his wedged clay ball at the same time as me. "You've done this before?"

"I was a baker," he replied, a little gruff, a little proud. "Back when it was all done by hand, not like those machines they use today."

"Well, I can see you must have been very good at it," Merrick said.

Clyde blushed and grumbled something, unable to take a compliment from anyone. "Here," I said, trying to hand him mine. "Do mine for me."

He dismissed me with a wave of his gnarled fingers. "I will bloody not. You can do it yourself."

I expected that response, but his grumpiness still made me chuckle. "You're a hard task-master."

I did manage to do the wedging-thing and get a somewhat ball-shaped lump of clay about the size of an orange. I liked how it felt in my hand. It was cool to the touch and heavy. A little damp and earthy. Because clay is earthy, I get that. But that was what I liked about it.

Merrick helped a few of the others, but soon we were all done. "Okay, so take it in your hand and we need to work it. Gentle," he said as he rolled it between his hands like he was making biscuits. Then he slapped it lightly. "Work it, tap it."

"That's also what he said," I whispered. Clyde nudged me with his elbow.

When I glanced at Merrick, I found him smiling at me. "But don't overwork it or you'll get cracks. Don't worry if it looks kind of rough. Pinch pots aren't always perfect."

My orange-sized ball of clay was far from perfect while Clyde's was a work of spherical art. "Look at you being all clever," I said, giving his clay a nod.

"We haven't even started yet. It's just a ball," Clyde said, his bushy eyebrows in a heavy line. He really hated compliments, which was why I loved giving them to him.

"Okay," Merrick said. He was standing at the end of the long table with Joan's clay ball in his hand. "I want you to hold the ball in your non-dominant hand."

I chewed on my bottom lip to stop myself from replying to that. Why was I suddenly twelve again? And why did Merrick smile at me like he knew?

He held the ball of clay up so we could all see it. "Holding the ball like so, push your thumb into it, nice and gentle, while supporting the weight. Push it in, nice and slow."

Oh, God.

Everyone else seemed to manage just fine, but I ducked my head so I wouldn't laugh, but my shoulders shook.

"You'll have to excuse Leo," Clyde said. "Dunno what's wrong with him today."

"I don't know either," I said, trying not to grin. Then I cleared my throat. "Sorry."

When everyone was busy *prepping* their clay, Merrick came over to me and pulled up the stool next to mine. I thought for a second I was going to get into trouble, but he was smiling. "Having fun?"

"I really am. I've been looking forward to this."

I pushed my thumb into the ball of clay, just like he'd shown us. "Careful not to go too far," he said, leaning in to look closer. "Now pinch it, or flatten it between your thumb and forefinger. Pinch turn, pinch turn. Yep, just like that," he said as I got the motion right.

"How you going with yours, Clyde?" I asked.

"Yeah, yeah, you just worry about your own," he groused.

I looked over and he already had a bowl shape forming. "Jeez, Clyde. You're making the rest of us look bad."

"You sure you haven't done this before?" Merrick asked.

"Never," Clyde replied.

"He worked with bread dough for fifty years."

"Fifty-seven years," Clyde corrected me.

"That explains why you're good with your hands then," Merrick said with a nod.

"That's what all the men say," I added with a bit of a laugh. "Ain't that right, Clyde?"

Clyde sighed and he looked right at Merrick. "I'd tell him to shove something in his mouth, but we all know how that'll end."

I laughed and Merrick did too. "Ignore those two," Shirley said from the end of the table. "Trouble, the both of them."

Clyde's gaze went to me and the corner of his mouth lifted in a smirk. "How's your pinch pot coming along, Shirley?"

"Just never you mind," she shot back curtly. Hers looked as bad as mine.

Clyde smiled at that, and I chuckled. "This was a really good idea," I said, just to Merrick. "Thank you for letting us come here."

His dark eyes were warm, as was his smile. "You're very welcome."

Yeah, okay. There was that pinging again. Though it really wasn't my gaydar. It was the look from him that made my heart thump against my ribs.

But we did manage to get our pinch pots into shape. I'm sure it took us twice as long as anyone else. Actually, Merrick could have probably done it in less than a minute, but we all laughed and chatted as he made his way around the table.

The thing was, this wasn't about being brilliant at pottery. This was about being social and having a good time, and that was something Merrick seemed to appreciate.

We got the little pinch pots done and wrote our initials on the bottom of them. Though I was certain no one was going to claim mine as theirs. We covered them to dry and put them into the drying room.

When the class was over, everyone thanked Merrick and promised to be back next week. And, oh yes, I was definitely coming back next week. In fact, I didn't even really want to leave now.

"Hey, Clyde. Want a cup of tea?" I asked. "My shout."

Clyde looked at me, then over to where Merrick was cleaning something in the sink. "Mm-hmm. Wouldn't be any other reason?"

I grinned at him. "I have no idea what you're talking about."

"Tea and scones and I won't tell him."

I gasped, audibly. "That's blackmail."

Now it was Clyde who grinned. "Isn't it beautiful?"

CHAPTER FOUR

MERRICK

OUR CLASSES WERE ALWAYS FUN, but this one was special. As they bickered and bantered, it was pretty clear they were all friends. Some were quieter than others, but they all contributed to the conversation and no one was left out. By the time the class was up, all the small pots were lined up, covered so they would dry evenly, and set aside for next week.

They all said goodbye and left in their pairs, but I noticed Leo and Clyde talking near the café. Clyde laughed at something and took a seat, and Leo shook his head as he went to the counter to order. I was tempted to go over and see what was so funny but wondered if it'd be weird if I intruded like that . . . I slid the tray of pots onto the bottom drying rack, and after I'd tidied up, I saw Ciara was carrying their order to their table. She chatted with them for a few seconds, the three of them smiling, and when Leo glanced my way, my feet were moving before my brain could stop me.

"Decided to stay, I see?" I said.

"Oh yes," Clyde said. "Leo here—"

Leo gave him a pointed glare.

"Leo owed me some scones and tea," Clyde continued. "We had a bet and I won. My clay pot was better than his."

I nodded thoughtfully. "Well, fair bet. It was."

Leo groaned. "He has an unfair advantage. The last time I did anything like that was in pre-school with Play-Doh."

"Merrick, can I get you your usual?" Ciara asked me.

"Uh." I hesitated. "Sure. Why not? If you guys don't mind the company?"

"Not at all," Leo answered, pulling out the chair next to him. Clyde seemed to find something about that amusing but he soon had a scone with jam and cream half shoved in his face. "This is an amazing set up you have here," Leo said. "The studio, the café. And you're the owner?"

"I am," I replied. "Well, between me and the bank, that is."

"Ugh, yeah. I can't even imagine." He sipped his tea. "How long have you been here?"

"Four years."

"That's amazing. And the interior design? With the exposed pipes and polished concrete floors. I love it."

"Thank you."

"I'm very impressed," he said, that mesmerising smile in place. "And I meant what I said before. I'm really glad we came along. Doing something like pottery had never crossed my mind, but I had the best time!"

"It was a great bunch of people. Do you guys do stuff as a group often?"

"Yep, once a week. It's usually something low-key and fun, and we don't always venture out, but this way Clyde and Shirley get to bicker somewhere different."

I laughed and looked over to Clyde. He'd finished one

scone and slowly got to his feet. "You okay, Clyde?" Leo said quickly, ready to stand.

"Just going to take a piss, Leo. Don't panic." When he walked past, he patted Leo's shoulder.

Leo smiled after him. "Sorry for the language."

"Don't worry about it. He seems like a great guy," I said, not wanting an awkward silence to fall over us.

"He is. He's a bit prickly and he grumbles about most things, but he's a real character."

"And the Bridge-the-Gap program?" I asked. "I'm very impressed with that."

"Yeah, it's great." Then he leaned in. "It's supposed to be for them—for the oldies—but I think we young'uns are the ones who get more out of it."

That made me laugh. "It's such a great concept. A lot of the older generation are excluded from our culture when it was them who paved the way."

"True," he replied. He smiled as he sipped his tea and gave me a curious look. "Our culture?"

"Yeah. Gay culture." I had a sinking feeling . . . "Oh, sorry, I assumed, and I shouldn't have. I just . . ."

"You think you wrongly assumed that I'm gay?" he asked. "Honey, I'm the gayest gay that ever gayed."

I laughed. "Is that like a Guinness Book of Records award?"

"Yep. I have the trophy and everything."

We both just sat there smiling for a bit. "I'm really glad your group came here today."

"Me too. The other options were swimming or knitting. Pretty sure Clyde would have tried to drown Shirley, and giving him knitting implements is asking for a grievous bodily harm incident."

I laughed. "So pottery was the safest option?"

"By far."

"I don't know whether to be offended or flattered."

"You should be flattered, for sure. I'm grateful, by the way. If Clyde went to swimming or knitting club, I'd be an accessory, so really, it's me who should be thanking you."

That made me laugh. "So how long have you and Clyde been partners in crime?"

"Two years."

"Wow."

"Yeah, we just clicked. In the beginning he wasn't too convinced. He thought I was going to be some young hoodlum." Leo shrugged. "He's come a long way. He never used to go out much, like he'd almost given up. He's been alone for a long time. His boyfriend died in the 80s. They'd been together for almost twenty years. He had no support, and he lost most of his friends to HIV."

"Jesus."

"Yeah. It's not a happy story. I'm just trying to bring a little light into his life."

"I think you're great," I said without realising how that sounded. "I mean, for doing what you do, and for helping him. That's great."

"No, you had it right the first time. I *am* great. It's a thing I am."

I laughed again but my smile faded. "I'm wondering if I should bring my uncle along next week. He's . . . He's gay but very . . . Not closeted exactly, but he's half Japanese and our family is somewhat traditional. He acknowledges that he's gay, and everyone knows, but he prefers not to flaunt it, or talk about it, or anything, really. He's very private . . ." I sighed. "He'd be horrified that I'm even talking about him, let alone if I told him the ceramics class was an LGBT group for seniors."

Leo's eyes softened. "I think it sounds like he might enjoy it. Gay men of that age tended to think they needed to be hidden away, which we know isn't the case anymore, but it's not easy for them. If he's not interested in ceramics, they do have the swimming and knitting. There's movie clubs and book clubs. They do bridge nights and even just coffee clubs. Jigsaws and crosswords, anything they want."

"Oh, he loves ceramics."

"Well, if you can convince him to come along, I'll make sure Clyde's on his best behaviour."

"I'll mention it, but I'm almost certain I know what the answer will be." I gave him a grateful smile. "Thanks."

"Anytime."

"Speaking of Clyde. He's been gone a while. Is he okay?"

"Oh yeah. He's totally giving me alone time with you. His subtlety needs some work."

I barked out a laugh. "Right. Well, then. Yes, I can't imagine he's subtle in anything he does."

"Like a sledgehammer."

"Not that I don't appreciate his effort, but should we go check on him or something?"

Just then, the bathroom doors opened and Clyde walked out, saw us both watching him, and waved his hand in front of his nose. "Might want to give that a while."

Leo groaned but it made me laugh. "I'll let you two finish your drinks in peace. I have another class starting soon; I better go get organised."

"Oh, okay. Sure," Leo said. "Thanks again, and talk to your uncle. He can only say no."

I stood up, taking my cup with me. "I will."

Clyde got to the table. "Don't be leaving on my account.

Should I go back to the bathrooms, Leo? But really, there's only so many tiles I can count."

I laughed again. I really liked Clyde, and I rather liked Leo too. "No, I have work to do, but thank you for the alone time with Leo."

He pulled out his seat and lowered himself into it, grumbling as he did. "Don't know what you're talking about."

I smiled at Leo. "I'll see you next Friday morning."

"I'm looking forward to it," he replied, his gaze firmly fixed on mine and killing me softly with that smile.

Me too, Leo. Me too.

CHAPTER FIVE

LEO

"WHAT DO you mean you didn't get his number?"

I felt buried under the weight of Clyde's disappointed stare, so I concentrated on driving instead. "Because I didn't."

"I left you alone with him for thirty minutes!" he exclaimed. "I took one for the team and you failed."

"It wasn't thirty minutes, it was more like ten—"

"Twenty."

"Ten. And anyway, I could call the studio if I had to get hold of him in some emergency situation. It's his business. So it wasn't a complete loss. And anyway, we don't do phone numbers first up. We do Grindr and Instagram."

Clyde ignored everything I'd just said. "I can't believe you crashed and burned."

"I didn't crash and burn. Or fail. I thought we had a bit of a connection. There was definite eye contact and smiling going on, and a little bit of flirting. He's gorgeous, don't you think?"

Clyde sighed. "You twenty-first-century gays are a strange lot."

I laughed as I pulled the car into a spot at Coles. "Come on, let's get these groceries done. Did you bring your shopping list?"

He pulled out a piece of paper from his pocket and unfolded it. The writing was shaky and large. I saw *bread* and *milk* before he folded it again. "Yep. All here."

I walked at his pace into the supermarket and grabbed a basket for him. I remembered how we'd once argued the pros and cons of fresh fruit over tinned. He was adamant that tinned peaches were just fine, but I tried to reason with him that fresh was best. We hadn't really been friends too long back then, and in hindsight, I should have known better. Tinned foods were cheaper, lasted longer, and were sometimes easier on arthritic hands, and my assumption that fresh was better for him was short-sighted and privileged. It was also not a mistake I made twice.

He was quiet as he picked up his usual brand of bread: the artisan, handmade kind. His bread was the only luxury he afforded himself because, as he'd explained a hundred times, that modern factory bread wasn't real bread. "I enjoyed today," he said softly, probably the most heartfelt thing he'd ever said to me. Then he, in typical Clyde form, added grumpily, "Not as much as you, though, even if you didn't get his number."

I grinned at him, my heart warming through. "I'm glad you enjoyed it."

"It's just like baking," he said. "Working the dough, or the clay. It's not too different."

"Hmm," I deadpanned. "If I knew you were going to be better at than me, I would have put us down for swimming."

He almost smiled. "Just be grateful it wasn't a baking class."

"Believe me, I am." I held out the basket while he put

some milk in. "I know you've told me about your being a baker, but seeing you with the clay today really showcased your skills."

"Bah." He dismissed me. "These old hands don't do what they used to."

"We should bake some bread at home," I said. I don't know why I didn't think of doing that before. "I'll bring all the ingredients over one time, and I can do the kneading, but you'll need to show me how."

Clyde stopped and gave me a flat look. "I saw your attempt at wedging and pinching clay, Leo. I just dunno if you're ready for bread. Or anything fit for human consumption, to be honest."

I laughed and pretended to search the breast pocket of my shirt. I reached in, pulled out my middle finger.

Clyde's face split in a grin. "I was also witness to your attempt at trying to sweet-talk the teacher. Not sure which was worse."

"Leave my little pinch pot alone. I'm going to finish him next week so he's perfect and sit him on my bookcase. He'll have pride of place in my flat."

He rolled his eyes and started up the next aisle. "God, help us all."

"Uh, next week," I hedged, falling into step beside him. "I don't even know if Merrick is single, or if he's just attentive to all new customers."

"If only you had his number."

"I'll search him up online when I get home. He'll be tagged in some of the studio pics, surely. I can follow those threads and see if there's an SO."

Clyde squinted; his caterpillar brows wiggled across his face. "I have no idea what you just said."

"Well, it's like getting a phone number but just . . . more twenty-first century. And SO means significant oth—"

"I know what that means." He grumbled as he shuffled up the aisle. "You better add some yeast to the basket if you're gonna torture me with your baking skills."

I smiled after Clyde. I wasn't kidding when I said I'd stalk Merrick out on social media to see if he was single or to see if he had any hidden nasties like racism or if he was part of some religious cult.

You know, all part of the usual twenty-first-century dating-criteria checklist of *hell no*.

I KICKED OFF MY SHOES, grabbed myself a bottle of water, and collapsed on the couch after work. My flatmate, Kell, sat opposite me and grinned. "Soooo," she said. "What did you find out? Is he single? Married? Is he a member of the Secret Spaghetti Monster's congregation?"

Kell and I had been living together for six years. We found each other when she'd advertised for a flatmate. She'd broken up with her then-girlfriend and needed someone to help pay the rent. I'd had a rather disastrous experience with my last flatmate and was looking for an alternative place to live. She advertised for an LGBTQ+ person in particular, I replied, and upon our first meeting, we had a conversation that kind of went like:

Her: Why are you looking for somewhere new? Did you not get along with your flatmate?

Me: We have different addictions. Mine is *RuPaul's Drag Race*, and his is cocaine and rent boys.

Her: Ew. Ew him, not ew *Drag Race*. Love that show.

Me: I know, right? Why are you looking for a new flatmate?

Her: I broke up with my girlfriend and she moved out.

Me: Oh no.

Her: Yeah. She made me watch *Where the Red Fern Grows*.

Me: *audible gasp*

Her: I know, right?

Me: That's just cruel.

Her: That's what I said! Then she told me to stop crying like a baby and to grow up.

Me: That bitch.

Her: When can you move in?

AND WE'D GOTTEN on like a house on fire ever since. We told each other everything and were truly like siblings. We could even pass for brother and sister, given our blond hair and blue eyes.

"Don't make me wait, Leo," she said. "I need all the details."

"Well, he's not married, and from what I can tell, he is single. There's no Grindr profile, which is a relief. No photos of him with another guy, no holiday snaps, and his Instagram is all about his pottery studio. He's been tagged in a few photos and seems to have a really cool group of friends. There's even a few family photos, and no crazy cult mentions, either."

"So basically you're saying that he is single and perfect."

"Pretty much, yep."

Kell laughed. "So, show me the pics." She nodded toward my phone.

I went straight to Instagram and found his profile. "Oh,

he's so cute!" She said. "Gotta love a guy who can put a rainbow flag in his profile."

"I know, right?"

She scrolled some more. "Did he make these?" They were two large, round ceramic bowls with some kind of crazy glaze. They were refined, minimalist but earthy, and they looked incredibly expensive.

"I think so. Pretty sure he only tags and watermarks his own stuff."

"Holy shit, he's clever."

"Uh . . . Holy shit he's gorgeous."

Kell laughed. "That too."

She scrolled down some more until she came to a photo of six friends at a table in a restaurant somewhere. There were empty plates and wine bottles on the table. They were all laughing, and Merrick had captioned it with "love these people." There were a few hashtags of friends and best friends, and they looked close and extremely happy.

Kell continued to scroll down through his posts until they found what looked like the grand opening of the studio. That was four years ago, and there was one photograph of Merrick inside his studio sitting at that long table, and he was laughing at something. It was a candid shot and strikingly beautiful. "Oh wow," Kell said.

And then she did the most horrifying thing anyone could ever do.

She accidentally double-tapped.

She looked at me, aghast. "Oops."

Holy flying shit balls. "What did you do?"

"I didn't mean to!" She squeaked and handed me back my phone like it was on fire. "Oh, Leo. I'm so sorry. So, so sorry."

I could literally feel the blood run from my face. She'd

just double-tapped. On his photo. She had just liked his photo from four years ago, on *my* profile! He was going to get a notification that basically proved I'd been stalking him. "Oh, this is bad. This is so bad."

"Maybe he doesn't check his notifications." She looked stricken. She pulled a couch cushion onto her lap and clung to it. "Maybe he doesn't use his Instagram much. Check when he posted his last photo; then see how often he posts at all. He might not ever know. He might not even know it's you."

"My profile picture is my face, with my name, and that I'm part of the Bridge-the-Gap program is in my bio."

"Oh God, Leo. I'm so sorry." Her face lit up then with an obvious idea. "Ooh, we can change your profile picture and your bio. Here, give me your phone. He'll never have to know."

"Or I could just move to Peru and become a llama farmer," I replied, not really joking. How was I going to face him on Friday? "Or maybe I can donate my body for organ harvesting a little sooner than expected."

"Ooh, dibs on your liver."

"Bitch, I need that."

Kell laughed. "Well, llama farming could be fun."

"I'll have to tell Clyde we're going to swimming instead of ceramics. If he ends up drowning Shirley, then I'll go to prison as an accessory which, to be quite frank, is preferable to facing Merrick on Friday morning."

Kell made a pained face. "I'll bake you cakes with nail files in them. I promise. If you go to jail, that is."

I patted her on the knee. "Thanks."

"It's probably the least I could do."

"Well actually, dinner is probably the least you could

do. Considering I now have to price some flights to Peru. Oh God, Kell. He's going to think I'm a stalker."

"I can do dinner," she said, nodding furiously. "What would you like? You name it."

"Carbohydrates and saturated fat. Pasta, pizza, ice cream. If I gain a hundred kilos in the next four days, he might not recognise me."

She laughed again but gave me a frown. "Oh, man. I really am sorry."

I sighed. "Well, what's done is done. I guess. Unless we go all Mission Impossible and steal his phone. If he hasn't seen it already."

Just then, my phone pinged with a notification. An Instagram notification, no less. It flashed on the screen so quick, and my adrenaline was so spiked I wasn't sure if I read the name correctly. My heart just about stopped! "Oh, God! I think that was him!"

"Quick, check it!" Kell cried, trying to peak at the screen. "What was it? Was it him?"

I opened the Instagram app, almost dreading what I would find. But there was Merrick's profile . . . "Oh, sweet Jesus, he liked two of my posts."

Kell's face almost split in half with her grin. "Oh my God! That is . . . You're welcome. That's what that is, thank you very much for the double-tap."

I laughed, relieved and amazed. "I can't believe he liked my posts. One when I'm with Clyde, and the other was the pancakes we made last week."

"The pancakes I made last week that you took credit for."

"Yeah, those."

"Well, crisis averted. You get to keep your liver and you

don't have to move to Peru, and Clyde doesn't have to drown Shirley."

But then something even more horrifying occurred to me. "Oh, holy shit balls. What do I do now?"

"You have to follow him!" Kell stated adamantly.

Oh God. I wanted to squeal and do some crazy dance but I was too chicken shit to even move. My phone buzzed again. "Oh, sweet mother of God, he just followed me."

Kell did the squealing happy dance on my behalf. I tapped the follow button right back, and a few seconds later, I had a message.

IS this the same Leo who is half of the Leo and Clyde super duo?

CHAPTER SIX

MERRICK

I DIDN'T NORMALLY HANG out on social media. I'd be lucky to post something a few times a week, and most of those were for the studio. Social media wasn't my forte, but I wasn't naïve enough to think that a business in today's market didn't need it. I'd post a photo of some latest creations or the café specials or if there was a new class starting. Occasionally I'd post pictures of people working with clay—with their permission, of course—to give the studio a human element.

And I just happened to be online when I saw one particular notification on my personal account. Someone had liked a photo of mine from a few years ago, which meant someone was scrolling through my profile . . .

I noticed his profile picture, then the name. *Leo by name, Pisces by nature.*

Leo was checking out my social media. It gave me a warm thrill, not gonna lie. I doubted he meant to double-tap my photo, but I was glad he did. I hadn't been able to get him out of my mind. Not just his looks or his laughter, and not even the way he looked at me like he was mentally undressing me. Which, admittedly, was nice . . .

But it was what he said that I couldn't get out of my mind. That some older gay men still believed they needed to be hidden away, and that was so true in the case of my uncle Donny.

Having that small group of gay seniors in my studio and hearing Clyde's story, and seeing them all with younger chaperones, really made me determined to invite my uncle Donny to come along. And there I was thinking I really didn't know where to start when I got an Instagram notification from someone who I could ask.

And it really didn't hurt when that particular someone was cute, funny, caring, and compassionate. And it *really* didn't hurt that he looked at me with those bedroom eyes.

I was certain it was him, but I sent off a quick message just to be sure.

Is this the same Leo who is half of the Leo and Clyde super duo?

His reply was quick. *It is. Super duo? Like Batman and Robin, or Celine Dion and Barbara Streisand?*

I laughed at my phone. *Depends. Can you sing?*

Trust me. You don't want Clyde and me to sing.

Crime fighters in tights it is, then.

Promise me you won't ever suggest that to Clyde . . . Is this the same Merrick who told me Clyde's pinch pot was better than mine?

I laughed again. *It is.* God, he was even cute and funny in messages. This was crazy, but what the hell . . . *Can I call you?*

There was no immediate reply, so he was either utterly horrified or trying not to sound too keen. I was hoping for the latter. I didn't want to scare him off or to make Friday's class awkward, so I typed out another message.

I have some questions about the bridge the gap program and my uncle. The phone call would be quicker than messages.

Oh sure, came his response. He sent through his phone number, and not wanting to sound completely desperate, I waited a good twenty seconds before I called him.

"Hello?"

I smiled at the sound of his voice. "Hi, it's Merrick. Thanks for taking my call."

"Oh, that's no worries. And just so you know, I was not the one who double-tapped your photo. It was Kell, she had my phone, so it looked like it was me but it wasn't."

"And who is Kell?"

"My flatmate."

"And she was checking out my Instagram because . . . ?"

"Well . . . because . . . Because we were stalking your profile. Ugh, sorry. That sounds creepy. It wasn't, I promise! I was showing her the ceramics studio because I haven't seen her all weekend, and I was telling her that the ceramics teacher was really cute and we were just catching up on the goss. You know how that is. So anyway, she took my phone and accidently double-tapped. It was horrifying, not gonna lie. I briefly considered moving to Peru. But we weren't being some crazy stalkers, I promise."

"You think I'm cute?"

"I think what?"

"You said that your ceramics teacher was really cute."

"I did not."

"Uh, yeah, you did."

"Christ. I'm gonna need those tickets to Peru. Do you know anything about llamas?"

I laughed again. I had no idea what he was talking about, but it was fun. "Not off the top of my head, no."

"Shame."

"I patted one once, at a wildlife park. Cute, but scary."

"How can something be cute and scary? Doesn't one cancel the other out?"

I chuckled. "It should. But there's anomalies in the animal kingdom."

Now he laughed. "I think you should name some."

Well, shit. "Llamas, because they spit. And geese."

"Geese?"

"Have you never encountered a goose?" I shuddered. "They're kinda cute and they waddle and honk, but seriously, they will fuck you up."

He burst out laughing. "Duly noted. Avoid geese at all costs."

"My uncle has a bird," I said, with no idea why. "It's only tiny. A little peach-faced lovebird. Anyway, it does this bouncing dance, which is cute. But hates people."

"Your uncle or the bird?"

"Uh, both." I laughed again. "Well, my uncle doesn't, really, but he doesn't handle crowds too well."

"Same."

"I thought you'd have loved crowds?"

"Me? Nah. Well . . ." He seemed to reconsider. "I will be the life of any party, like I'm a lead-the-revolution kind of guy, but then I'll need a week or two where I don't see another person outside of work and my flatmate."

That made me smile. "Can relate."

"It's not easy when you work in the service industry. I work retail in the city, so . . . well, yeah. When it comes to the general public, I'm jaded and cynical, and believe me, there is nothing I haven't seen."

I snorted out a laugh. "Sounds gross."

"It's worse than the Pump House on a Friday night . . ." He trailed off. "Uh, you don't frequent The Pump House, do you? Because I didn't mean—"

"Uh, God, no." The Pump House was a venue aimed at gay men. The kind of club where questionable clientele leave their manners at the door. Where your feet stuck to the floor, and you didn't go into the back rooms without a hazmat suit and a vat of antibacterial gel. "Not since I was eighteen."

"Wow. Baptism of fire."

"There was a group of us, and we thought we'd check it out. It was eye-opening, that's for sure. Like if Porn Hub was a venue and not a website." I also had no idea why I said that. I mean, it wasn't a lie, but mentioning porn in our second-ever conversation wasn't really like me.

I was relieved when he laughed again. "I'm afraid I don't know what you mean. You'll have to explain. In vivid, *vivid* detail, please."

Thank God he laughed it off and didn't think I was all about sex. "Another time, perhaps. Like maybe our third conversation. You know, don't want you to think I'm weird or anything."

"That train left the station with the llamas and the geese."

I snorted again. "The llama conversation was all you. You're the one who mentioned Peru."

"It's been an eventful conversation, hasn't it?"

"Enlightening."

"So did you actually have a question about the Bridge-the-Gap program and your uncle?" he asked. I could picture him smiling as he spoke. "Or was that a ruse to hear my sexy voice?"

Oh shit, the questions, yes. "I almost forgot. I mean your voice is great and all, but yes, I do."

I paused and he waited. "Are you going to ask me the question? Or is this some game of charades? Which I hope it's not because I hate to break it to you, Merrick. I can't actually see you right now. Are you doing hand signals? How many syllables?"

I chuckled. "No, I'm not playing charades. Though I would totally kick your arse if we were. I have serious skills."

"Serious charade skills. Is that a challenge? Because that sounds like a challenge. But before you agree, you should know I too have a talent for charades. And Pictionary. I have quite a few hidden talents. For board games," he added quickly. "God, that could have got awkward."

That made me chuckle. I could so easily have replied with some sexual innuendo about the talents to which he referred, but I thought I should keep it light. "Not as awkward as my porn comment earlier, so we're even. And anyway, I think I'll need a reference point for your talents because I've seen your attempt at making a pinch pot."

He gasped. "Don't image-shame my pinch pot. He can't help how he looks."

I laughed, grateful he wasn't offended by my comment. "I'm just kidding, by the way. You actually did pretty good."

"Aw, thanks."

"Not as good as Clyde's, but still . . ."

"That's it. Clyde's not coming back. I can't let him show me up like that."

He sounded as though he was still smiling but I needed him to know I was only joking. "Please bring Clyde back. I really liked him. And that's kind of what I wanted to ask you about."

"Oh God, did he offend someone again? Did Shirley complain? Because those two bicker like old hens. Not that I think she would complain. Was it Harvey?"

"No, no one complained. Actually, everyone said they loved it."

"Well, thank goodness for that," Leo replied. "Because once I took him to a cooking-for-seniors class and, I'm not even kidding, but the first lesson was bread. And oh boy, that didn't end well. The guy teaching the class wouldn't know how to prove yeast if it rose up and smacked him in the nads, apparently. And anyway, after Clyde suggested the teacher sprinkle some yeast between his ears to see if his brain could grow, it was kind of suggested that we not come back."

I snorted out a laugh. "He's passionate about his bread, huh?"

"That's putting it mildly." He sighed cheerfully. "Okay, so no one was offended, no one complained; that's a good day for Clyde. What did you want to ask me about him?"

"I want to bring my uncle along to the next session, and I was kind of hoping Clyde could put in a good word about the program."

"You want to put your uncle near Clyde? On purpose?"

I chuckled. "Yes."

"Well, just so you know, if offending people was a sport, he'd be at the Olympics. Not even kidding. He's brusque, grumpy, and sometimes he's just downright rude."

I grinned. "Perfect."

CHAPTER SEVEN

LEO

I DISCONNECTED the call with Merrick, confused but happy. We'd spoken for forty minutes, and by the time we were done, Kell had spaghetti Bolognese cooked, and she was sliding two plates onto the small round dining table in the corner. I grabbed our drinks, but she was staring at me as I sat down.

"Well, look at you."

"Look at me, what?"

"Your smile." She picked up her fork and pointed it at me. "You two were chatting for ages. Spill the deets."

"We did speak for ages, didn't we?" I couldn't help but grin, and possibly do a little wiggle in my seat. "He's so witty and smart. And cute. I made him laugh, so that's gotta be a good sign, right? And it was a good laugh. Like, he was laughing with me, not at me. So that's always a good thing."

"True."

"What does he want to do with Clyde?" she pressed. "I wasn't exactly eavesdropping, but I heard that part."

The thing about our flat was that it was hard not to hear each other's phone conversations, so I didn't mind that she'd heard. "He wants to bring his uncle along to the next ceramics lesson."

Kell swirled some spaghetti onto her fork. "Isn't it his studio? He can bring whoever he wants."

"No, as part of the class. But just unofficially. Merrick wants to get him involved in the Bridge-the-Gap program, to let him see how it can be fun. But he said if he suggested it outright, he knows his uncle would refuse. But if he comes along, he might see it's not so bad."

She swallowed her food. "That's actually kind of sweet."

I shoved in a mouthful, chewed, and swallowed. "It is. He is, sweet, that is. And Kell, this spag-bol is really good."

She grinned. "Thanks."

"Anyway, Merrick asked if I could word Clyde up a bit, that there'll be a new participant, and maybe if he could make him feel welcome."

She stared, unblinking. "Clyde?"

I snorted. "I know."

"Gee. What could possibly go wrong?"

I took another mouthful and it at least hid my smile as I chewed. "I could list a possible hundred different scenarios of all the ways it could go wrong, actually. And come this Friday, we'll find out."

"He'll be fine," Kell said with a smile. "Clyde will be a true gentleman, just you watch."

"WHAT DO you mean I gotta babysit?" Clyde barked. "I ain't no babysitter, Leo. Christ. Does he need someone to hold his hand everywhere he goes?"

I held the lobby door open and waited for a grouchy

Clyde to walk through. "It's not babysitting. He's not a child. He's a grown man."

"That's worse!"

"He's not a grown man who needs babysitting. There is no babysitting. Merrick just thought it might be nice to get his uncle out and about, that's all. And that he would enjoy the Bridge-the-Gap program if he could just see how fun it was. He doesn't get out much, apparently. Remember what that was like?"

Clyde stopped walking to the car so he could frown at me. He huffed and grumbled something before he began walking again. "Fine."

"If he likes it, he might join the program. He might prefer the movie club or swimming. I dunno." I opened the passenger side door for Clyde. "And, although I don't know why, Merrick liked you and thought you were funny." I waited for Clyde to get himself into the car, then shut the door. I hurried around the driver's side, eager to get to the studio. Well, eager to see Merrick. Who was I kidding?

Clyde huffed and puffed for the first few blocks. "So, you spoke to this Merrick fella. Didn't think you had his number."

"I didn't. At first." How did I explain all this to Clyde so it made sense? "Long story short, I found him on social media and accidently liked a photo of his. He recognised my profile picture and messaged me. We got chatting and exchanged phone numbers."

"Sounds complicated."

"Meeting and dating in the twenty-first century," I replied.

"That's where all you young'uns go wrong. You need to start courting again."

"Courting?" I laughed. "Jeez, today's version of courting is swiping right."

"Swiping what?"

"Never mind."

"You need more romance, more spark."

I smiled as I pulled up to a stop at a set of lights. "Sounds nice. Is that what you used to do? Did you court John, or did he court you?"

It wasn't often we talked about John. His lover had died a long time ago, but he'd never really gotten over it, and bringing his name up in conversation wasn't easy. But I wanted Clyde to know he could talk to me about John.

Clyde shot me a bit of a look, but he turned his attention back out the front of the car and raised his chin. "He courted me."

"I bet he did," I added. "I've seen those photos of you being all sexy back in your heyday."

Now Clyde groused and shook his head as though I was being ridiculous. "Things were different back then. We weren't out in the open like you guys are now. We'd sometimes take my sister and her friend to the pictures with us so we didn't look suspect. But we'd drive around in his car or hang out at the beach, because guys did that." Clyde smiled as his eyes went to some far distant memories. "But he'd write me poetry, and we'd listen to the wireless radio and hold hands." He sighed. "Probably sounds stupid to you."

"Sounds perfect to me."

He managed a bit of a smile. "It took us six months of skirting around each other before either of us worked up the courage to act interested. I was so scared he'd be offended and have a bunch of guys beat me up, and it turned out he was just as scared. But it's all in the eyes. You can't hide that look." It was a rare moment from Clyde, and I almost regretted pulling up at the ceramics studio. I wanted to know more.

"Was there a brush of fingers or an innocent touch?" I asked. "All that courting romance?"

Clyde shook his head. "Nope. We went to the Valley Baths and had to change into our trunks. He walked into my change room when I wasn't quite finished getting my togs pulled all the way up. He froze, I froze, with my trunks around my thighs, mind you. He . . . liked what he saw and locked the door behind him."

I grinned at him. "Did he help you get your swimming trunks on?"

"Not right away." He winked.

I burst out laughing. "That's my favourite story of yours yet."

He was quiet for a moment, then he nodded to the studio across the small car park. "Well, we better get inside so you can flounder all over the handsome teacher. You're not going to do anything to embarrass me, are ya?"

"Like what?"

"Incoherent babbling or gaping like a stunned fish. That kind of thing."

God, I hope not. I grinned at him. "I'll do my very best." I got out and waited for him to do the same. Moving at Clyde's pace was actually refreshing. No rushing, no crazy schedules or pressure of the world to have and do everything now, now, now. Slowing down every once in a while wasn't a bad thing.

So if it took Clyde a little longer to get out of the car and cross the street, then I would wait. I didn't mind one bit.

I held the door for him and smiled as he shuffled through, grumbling as he went. "Suppose we'll be having more tea and cake afterwards too," he said.

"With a bit of luck," I replied, following him in.

He hobbled through the small café into the ceramics studio. Shirley saw him first. "Nice of you to turn up. Running late again, I see."

It was a typical jibe, one they'd traded many times. Only this time Clyde didn't fire back. He was distracted, staring, gaping like a fish at a man sitting on a stool by the sinks, by the huge windows along the back wall. He was an older Asian man, small-framed, and had short, straight grey hair. Merrick was standing beside him and they were talking quietly, and sure, Merrick was better looking today than he had been the week before—the way the sunlight glowed around him was kinda magical—but I couldn't take my eyes off Clyde.

He was stuck, his mouth open, cheeks flushed. If he were a cartoon, he'd have hearts in his eyes. And I would never claim to be any kind of expert, but I knew smitten at first sight when I saw it.

CHAPTER EIGHT

MERRICK

UNCLE DONNY WASN'T HAPPY. He didn't want to come to a pottery class, he didn't want anything to do with the Bridge-the-Gap program, and he didn't want to meet the other attendees. He hated meeting new people; he hated being put on the spot.

But like all self-serving nephews, I'd dealt a pretty low blow. "Do it for me, please," I'd said, knowing he then wouldn't refuse. But I also knew there was a very good chance he might enjoy himself if he came along, if he just gave it a chance.

So he sat by the sink, physically as far away from the others as the studio allowed. "I'm doing this for you," he reminded me quietly. "Though please don't make a fuss of my being here."

"I won't," I promised. I looked up to see Leo and Clyde walking in. My chest tightened, butterflies swarmed my belly. It was ludicrous, but I liked Leo. Well, I could find myself liking him. After our phone conversation in which we talked effortlessly for ages, I was nervous to see him today. I didn't want the bubble of possibility to burst.

I was hoping I could maybe score a coffee date after today.

"Ah, I see," Uncle Donny said. He glanced from me to Leo and back again. "The pretty boy has caught your eye. Is that why I'm here? To act as a conversation point?"

I laughed. My quiet-spoken, painfully introverted, seventy-year-old uncle was my wingman. "Not exactly. Well, maybe a little bit. He is cute though, right?" Uncle Donny raised an eyebrow at me, so I shrugged. "Well, we can't put it off forever," I whispered. True to his wishes, I needed to introduce him without much fanfare. "Good morning everyone," I greeted the class. "If you could please come up to the drying room and find your pinch pot."

They each stood up and did as I'd asked, and while they were taking their time and chatting, I led Uncle Donny to the end of the table, to where Leo and Clyde were standing, waiting for the others to go first.

"Hi," Leo said. He bit his bottom lip as though he was trying not to smile too hard. His cheeks flushed pink.

"Hey," I replied, sure my face was doing similar things to his.

Leo looked to Uncle Donny and gave me a nod. "Clyde, I'll grab your pinch pot. You sit back down." He walked off with a knowing smile.

"Clyde, this is my uncle, Donny. I thought he might like to join you and Leo today. If that's okay with you?"

It was then I noticed that Clyde was a little red in the face and flustered.

"You okay, Clyde?" I asked.

He snapped out of what daze he was in and pulled out the chair next to his. "Yes, oh yes, please take a seat. Where are my manners? Of course it's okay."

Uncle Donny gave me a cautionary glance, but he took

the seat and Clyde helped him push it in closer to the table. And once Uncle Donny was comfortable, Clyde patted down his own hair, then took his own seat. Was he nervous? Flustered?

Oh.

Leo came walking back with their pinch pots but he was grinning and gave a nod to Clyde. Thankfully no one else had really seemed to notice Clyde's reaction too much and I didn't want to be the one to bring it to their attention. Shirley gave him enough grief as it was, all good-naturedly, of course. But I wanted to protect Clyde from ridicule, if I could. And from the possibility of drawing unnecessary attention to Uncle Donny. Though I did have to introduce him; better me, making it quick, than the whole table making a deal out of it.

"Everyone, this is my uncle, Donny. He'll be joining us today," I said, quick and to the point, followed by a sharp change in subject. "Today we'll be applying any patterns you might want before we add glaze to your pinch pots and get them ready for the kiln."

I gave Uncle Donny the pot I'd made last week and showed the class how to etch patterns with tools, and then we sorted through glazes. I helped everyone with any patterning they wanted, and conversation filled the table. When everyone was busy, I pulled up a seat beside Leo. "How's the glaze coming along?" I asked quietly.

He made a face at his very grey glaze. "Are you sure this is blue?"

I laughed. "Promise. It oxidises in the kiln."

He gave a quick, pointed glance toward my uncle. "Your uncle's here. You must have been convincing."

"Emotional blackmail."

He chuckled. "Whatever works."

I spared Uncle Donny and Clyde a quick look. Clyde was pointing to something on Uncle Donny's pinch pot, and my uncle was . . . smiling?

"This is unexpected?" Leo whispered.

"Very," I replied with a smile to Harvey's work. "Looks really good, Harvey."

Leo held out his pinch pot. "Not as pretty as mine."

A few others laughed, and I did too because, really, Leo's pinch pot was a lot of things, but pretty was not one of them. It was rough, uneven, a little lopsided. But much like its maker, it was cute and totally charming.

Leo made a point of ridiculing himself, laughing and talking to the others, making himself the centre of attention, and I was almost certain he did it to keep the attention away from Clyde and Uncle Donny. It was sweet, and I really liked that he did that.

He looked particularly cute today. He wore another tropical button-down shirt with short sleeves and denim cut-off shorts. But sitting beside him, I got to see the laugh lines at the corner of his eyes and how utterly perfect his profile was when he laughed. He also smelled particularly good, and I could only imagine running my nose up his neck to his jaw, just to see how his scent lingered there.

That thought struck me out of my daydream, and I caught Shirley watching me and no doubt seeing the way I was looking at Leo. She gave me a small, knowing smile before turning back to her glazing. She dabbed her pinch pot with a paintbrush, quickly joining in on a conversation as though she hadn't just seen me fawning all over Leo.

My cheeks heated, though thankfully no one seemed to notice.

"What do you think?" Leo asked. I hadn't exactly heard

what he was talking about, but he was gesturing to his pinch pot expectantly. Proudly, even. It just made him cuter.

"I think it's great," I replied.

He beamed and I ignored the way Shirley smiled at me. But it was a good reminder to move forward with their lesson. "Okay, so if we're all done, we'll get cleaned up and start on the bowls. We only need to roll the clay and shape it today, ready for next week."

"We don't get to put them in the kiln?" Joan asked.

"No. I'll have them done later this afternoon after another class," I explained. "There'll be a few more things to go in it yet, and the kiln takes a while. I'll have them ready for you next week."

Everyone took their pinch pots back into the drying room, and I was surprised to see Uncle Donny carry Clyde's for him. Uncle Donny didn't look at me, of course, keeping his chin raised and his gaze cast straight ahead. Leo grinned at me as he followed him in, and it was hard not to smile in return.

I then had everyone sit back at the table and gave them each a lump of clay. I reminded them how to wedge the clay before I brought out two thin dowels and a rolling pin. Then, putting the clay between the two rods, I began rolling it out and I told them what diameter we needed. "The rods will only allow me to roll the clay to the perfect thickness so it stays even."

They each had their own thin dowels and a rolling pin, and it took no time at all. Uncle Donny had done this a hundred times and it was pretty obvious Clyde had too. His bakery skills were proved once again, whereas Leo needed a little more help.

He kept pushing his rods away with his rolling pin and his clay had somehow ended up with thumbprints and two knuckle marks. Clyde took one look at it and shook his head. "Excuse me, Merrick. I think Leo needs some help." Leo had the audacity to look offended, but Clyde just winked at him. "I'm your wingman, remember?"

I baulked because I'd only earlier thought of my uncle as the same. I glanced at Leo to see if he'd noticed my reaction, but he was too busy blushing. "Oh, excellent! Thanks for announcing that. It's not embarrassing at all."

I laughed, relieved, but didn't mind helping Leo one bit. And it would seem Leo didn't mind it either. I certainly didn't mind standing that close and brushing elbows and catching that hint of aftershave again.

"Sorry about that," Leo whispered. "I would have asked Clyde, but he's busy helping your uncle."

I looked over, and sure enough, Uncle Donny was letting Clyde roll out and turn the clay. I bit back a smile. "Don't tell Clyde, but Uncle Donny could do that with his eyes closed. I think my uncle is a little taken with him."

Leo's smile was breathtaking. "I think Clyde is a little taken too."

I met his gaze, and my heart beat a mile a minute. This was so crazy. "Can you stay for a coffee after class?"

His smile somehow got even better. "Sure."

I laughed with relief, sure he could probably hear my heart hammering at my ribs.

"Um, Merrick?" Joan was frowning at her clay, obviously needing some help with it, which was a great distraction. Once we were all done, I put the stack of plastic bowls onto the work table.

"We're going to use these as moulds. We'll line the bowls with our sheets of clay and press them into shape. Next week, they'll be dry and hard enough to pattern and glaze."

"Isn't that cheating?" Shirley asked. "Shouldn't we have to build it?"

"No, it's not cheating, per se," I replied. "We're . . . using the tools we have at hand." I pulled the bowls apart. There were cereal bowls, rice bowls, salad bowls, some round, some more square. "There's a few different shapes, and they've all been used before and will be used again. I bought them for about fifty cents each at a clearance sale, so don't worry too much about making a mess of them."

They each chose a bowl and carefully lined it with their sheet of clay, pressing it in nice and firm. We wrapped them in plastic and they stored them away in the drying room for next week, and just like that, all too soon, the class was finished.

They all chatted for a bit, some playfully bickering, though they mostly laughed. There was, I noticed, a slight change in the dynamics between Shirley and Clyde. He wasn't being snarky to her, and she wasn't biting him back. As the conversation moved on, Uncle Donny and Clyde had moved off and were standing at the huge window. I couldn't hear what they were saying but Uncle Donny was pointing to something outside—a plant or tree probably— and he was doing all the talking while Clyde listened intently. As everyone else was leaving, though, Shirley winked at Leo. "He's on his best behaviour, isn't he? Should have tried to set him up years ago."

Leo laughed her off and told her to have a good weekend. Eventually, thankfully, we were alone. "Coffee? Or tea?" I asked Leo quietly. "I think we should leave those two to chat."

He nodded and we slipped into the café to a table closest to the studio so Clyde would be able to see Leo from where they stood.

I ordered our drinks and Ciara gave me a smile punctuated with a less-than-discreet eyebrow wiggle. "Take a seat. I'll bring them over," she said.

"Can you believe those two?" Leo asked excitedly as I sat beside him.

"I seriously cannot," I replied. "My uncle doesn't talk to people. Like, at all. This is a milestone. And completely unexpected."

"Well, I don't know how much talking he got in during the class. I think Clyde did most of the talking."

"My uncle doesn't say much." I glanced over at them again, making sure they couldn't hear. They were well out of earshot. Uncle Donny was still explaining something, in great detail, it would seem. "But he sure is talking now."

Leo chuckled. "I can't believe how well-behaved Clyde was. And you know what's funny?" he asked. "On the way over here in the car, I told how we'd spoken on the phone, and he was like, 'Don't you get in there and gape like a fish,' which I would never do. But oh my God, he took one look at your uncle and was absolutely gobsmacked. He was the one gaping like a fish out of water. As soon as he laid eyes on him. I thought he might have recognised him, but no. He was just agog."

"Agog?"

"Yep. One hundred per cent agog."

"I wasn't aware that agog was still a word."

"Oh yeah, it sure is. In fact, if you googled it, there would probably be a picture of Clyde's face when he first saw your uncle."

I chuckled, but something he said stuck in my mind. "You told Clyde we spoke on the phone?"

"Sure." He shrugged and blushed a little. "We talk

about everything. I told you he was mad at me for not getting your number last week."

"Um." I tried to recollect. We'd talked for a while on the phone, but I was pretty sure I'd remember that. "No, you didn't tell me that."

He blanched. "Oh, I didn't? Um, that's not embarrassing." He made a face, then settled on a shrug. "Well, he was. Mad at me, that is."

"You wanted my phone number after your lesson last week?"

"Well, not directly," he said, blushing down his neck. "I mean, I certainly wouldn't have minded. But remember how Clyde made a point of going to the bathroom for a really long time last week to give us some alone time?"

"Yeah?"

"Well, apparently that was so I could get your phone number. He was kinda pissed that I didn't."

"Oh."

"He said I was a disgrace to gay men everywhere."

"Wow. Harsh."

"You've met Clyde, right? Everything he says is harsh."

I chuckled. That might have been true, but looking at him with my uncle, it didn't seem that way. Ciara brought our coffees over, smiled a little too widely, but thankfully didn't linger.

"Anyway," Leo continued. "In the car earlier, I mentioned that we had spoken on the phone. He told me not to embarrass him and not to be all agog when I saw you." He sipped his coffee, then said, "Which is actually kinda horrifying and I can't believe I just told you that."

I grinned at him. "I don't mind. You already told me on the phone you think I'm cute, so being a little agog is allowed."

He groaned and he blushed so hard the tips of his ears went red. "Technically, I didn't tell you that directly. I told Kell that the ceramics teacher was cute. I was just relaying the information to you second hand."

"Oh, right. That makes sense."

"Does it?"

"Not really." I laughed. God, he was so funny. "If it's any consolation, as the aforementioned ceramics teacher, I think it's only fair I say that there is a cute guy who comes in on a Friday morning. He wears bright floral shirts and he makes me laugh."

Leo grinned again. "Are you knocking my shirts?" He looked down at it. "This is one of my favourites."

It was covered in green fronds with pink flowers. "No, I like them. They're bright and cheery. And you have a great sense of style, obviously."

"Thank you. But I work at Cotton On. Not exactly thrilling work, but I enjoy fashion so I kind of love my job. And it helps that I know how to coordinate a wardrobe."

"God, you would probably die if you saw mine. Everything I own is covered in clay. Or glaze, or dust. Or . . ." I looked down at my clothes. I was wearing an apron, but the stains on my sleeves were still visible.

"I like your wardrobe," he said, then made a face. "Well, I mean. What I've seen you wear the whole two times I've seen you. Business shirts or linen shirts are classic. Very stylish."

"Oh." My cheeks heated again. "Um, thanks? But honestly, I put zero thought into this."

"So you can look a million dollars with zero effort. Noted." He smiled as he sipped at his coffee.

My blush deepened, my cheeks burned. There was definitely something brewing between us. That excitement, that tangible energy, the looks that induced butterflies. I licked my lips. "So, did you enjoy your class today?"

"Hell yes. I love this. I love the pottery, I love this studio, I love the Bridge-the-Gap program and the folks that come along every week." He nodded toward where Clyde and Uncle Donny were still talking. "And that right there is so great. I can't even explain it."

I watched my uncle smiling for a second before I grinned at Leo. "It really is."

"Do you think your uncle will come back next week? He seemed to enjoy it today."

"I hope so."

"Do you think they'll see each other again?" Leo asked. "Do you reckon they've lined up a hot date?"

That made me laugh. "I have no idea, but I sure hope so."

"Me too."

Just then, Uncle Donny shot a look toward me, then looked to the floor. Clyde said something, and with a nod and a smile, he began to walk over toward us. Uncle Donny began cleaning up the sink area.

Leo put the coffee cup to his lip. "Well, here he comes."

This was my last moment alone with him . . . I had three seconds, tops. "Would you have dinner with me?" I asked.

Leo almost choked on his coffee. He put the cup down, then wiped his chin, and was now a delicious shade of pink. "Oh, uh, yes. Sure. Of course. I mean, yes please. God. Um, when?"

He was just so freaking adorable. "Tonight?"

His grin was nothing short of spectacular. "Tonight would be great."

Clyde arrived at our table, his expression unreadable. "We ready to go, Leo?"

"Oh." Leo stood quickly. "Yeah, sure. Everything okay?"

"Just done for today," he replied and began walking toward the door.

Leo gave me an apologetic frown. "I'm sorry."

"Don't apologise."

"But tonight, yes?"

"I'll text you later."

He smiled, threw a ten-dollar note from his pocket. "That's for the coffee."

Before I could argue, he was gone, helping Clyde out the front door. I smiled because, holy hell, I'd scored a date with Leo tonight! But wondering what might have soured Clyde's mood, I turned to where Uncle Donny was now wiping down the tabletop. I took our cups back over to the counter and left the tenner with Ciara. "Did things with the cutie in the floral shirt not go well?" she asked. "You both smiled like things were going well."

"No, he was great. His name is Leo, and he's . . . great." I tried to rein in my smile. "I have a date with him tonight, actually."

"You do?" Her eyes were wide, but then she looked confused. "So why the long face?"

"We thought my Uncle Donny and Clyde, Leo's buddy, were . . . you know, getting along. But maybe not. Clyde didn't look too happy when he left."

"Oh no." She sympathised with a frown.

"I better go see what's wrong," I said. Then, with a heavy sigh, I made a beeline toward my uncle.

CHAPTER NINE

LEO

I WAITED until we'd crossed the street, then I waited until we were buckled in, and then I waited until I'd driven a block. "Everything okay?"

He reached into his top pocket and pulled out a piece of paper. "One phone number. And that, my young friend, is how it's done."

Wait, what?

"You got his phone number?"

"I sure did."

I laughed. Like really laughed. Surprised and amazed. "But you looked miserable when you left . . ."

"We couldn't have you and Donny's nephew making things awkward. Donny's not big on public attention."

"Merrick said as much. But you sly old dog. A phone number? After meeting him once!" I couldn't help but grin. "You are one smooth operator." Then something occurred to me. "Hey, wait up. I was just getting to the interesting part with Merrick when you needed to leave."

"But you have his number, right?"

"Well, yes." I stopped at the lights. Then gave him a cheeky smile. "And I also have a date with him tonight."

He shot me a look; a slow smile spread across his face. "Who asked who?"

"He asked me."

"A good sign."

"I hope so. Who asked who in your phone number exchange?"

"I asked him," Clyde said.

"Good for you."

"He's . . . he was . . ." Clyde shook his head and his voice was quiet. "He's one of the most beautiful men I've ever seen."

I was about to burst. Not even kidding. I thought I might burst in the car and explode like a balloon filled with paint, covering the inside of my car with my innards. "Oh, I'm so happy for you."

"Yeah well," he replied, clearly remembering his grumpy demeanour. "Not gonna get myself all tied up in knots about anything just yet. Cool your jets there, boy. It's been a long time for me."

Pretty sure there would be no cooling of jets. "Isn't that more of a reason to let yourself be excited about it now?"

Clyde's scowl gave way to an almost smile. "Yeah, yeah. So tell me, what have you planned for your date tonight?"

"I don't know. Because you interrupted us."

He didn't even look one bit sorry. He just smiled out the windscreen. "I got his phone number . . ."

And I couldn't even be mad. So I sang Sade's "Smooth Operator" all the way to his house. And he didn't even tell me to shut up once.

NOT WANTING to appear too desperate, I waited almost three hours before I texted Merrick.

Hey, sorry Clyde interrupted us before we could discuss it. Did you still want to do something tonight?

His reply came back a whole eight minutes later. *Yes, for sure. There's an open cinema night in the park at New Farm tonight. I think they're playing* E.T. *Is that cool or stupid?*

I laughed. *100% cool.*

Oh thank God. I thought so too. Dinner first?

My answer to food is always yes.

Greek, Lebanese, Korean?

Yes.

LOL. Can I pick you up around six?

Sure. I was pretty sure he had my address anyway, because I'd had to fill in all mine and Clyde's details when we enrolled for the program at his studio. I texted him my address regardless. *See you at six.*

See you then.

I put my phone down, fully aware I was grinning like an idiot but unable to stop it. If he was going to pick me up at six and Kell got home at about five thirty, that meant I'd have to tell her everything the second she walked in. Because, holy shit, I had a date with Merrick tonight! I considered texting her, but there was no way she could reply while she was at work.

I fell onto the couch with a happy sigh and looked around the lounge room. It wasn't exactly tidy . . . And it wasn't likely that Merrick would see the inside of our flat tonight, was it? I hadn't said if I'd meet him out the front or if he'd come in first. And holy shit, what if he came home with me after the movie?

I shot off the couch and tidied everything, straightened cushions and cleaned up the kitchen. I even cleaned the toilet. But I got to my room and stopped. I was not stripping the bed. I absolutely wasn't. Because there was no way, absolutely no way he would be seeing the inside of my bedroom on our first date. It was highly unlikely he'd even see the inside of my flat, let alone the inside of my bedroom, and most definitely not in my bed.

I didn't want just *one* night with him. I wanted more than that. And I wanted him to want more . . .

Oh God, what if he didn't want more?

I heard a key in the door and whipped out my phone to check the time. No way. I'd been cleaning for hours? And I still hadn't showered!

Kell came through the door looking ever so glad it was Friday. "Oh, I've never been more grateful . . ." Her words died away. "What?"

I must have been staring.

Then she looked around the flat. "Have you been cleaning? Jeez, Leo, the place is sparkling."

"I have a date," I blurted out. "With Merrick!"

She blinked. "What?"

"I lost track of time. He's going to be here in half an hour to pick me up."

"He's picking you up? Like a gentleman? Oh my God, Leo, that's so cute," she cooed, excited and giddy. Then her eyes went wide. "Half an hour?"

I nodded. She pointed to the bathroom. "Shower. Now. You're all sweaty and smell like Spray and Wipe. Unless lemon household cleaner mixed with sweat is the scent you're going for." I made an *ewww* face and she pointed harder at the bathroom. "Leo, shower. Make it quick! I need details before you leave."

"Oh God, do I need to shave?" I felt my jaw.

"I don't know. Does he like stubble?"

"I don't know. We haven't got that far yet."

"Does he have stubble?"

"Yes."

"Well, I'd say you should shave."

"Just because he has stubble himself doesn't mean he doesn't like it on other guys."

"Leo, this is a truly riveting chat and all, but you're wasting time." She pushed me toward the bathroom, then pulled her hand away. "God, you're all sweaty. That's gross."

"Okay, okay, I'm getting in the shower." I shut the bathroom door behind me and pulled off my shirt.

"Thanks for cleaning the flat though," Kell called out. "Looks great."

I turned the water on and stripped off completely. At least we don't have to do it tomorrow now, I thought. Though I did have to be at work early, which was going to suck. Depending on how tonight went, of course.

Don't think about it, Leo. Don't overthink it.

I had the quickest shower of my life, even managing a quick shampoo. I dried off quickly, tied the towel around my waist and dashed into my room, only to be surprised by Kell at the foot of my bed. I let out the manliest high-pitched scream ever while clutching my towel. Kell didn't even bat an eyelid; she nodded toward my bed. "I picked out your clothes for you. So you didn't have a meltdown and waste time. I'd hate for Merrick to knock on the door and I'd have to tell him you can't go out tonight because you're sobbing on the floor in front of your wardrobe."

Sure enough, there was an outfit laid out on the bed. "I can't decide if I should be offended or thankful," I said.

"I've seen your meltdowns—"

"No, not about that," I clarified. We both knew what

she said was true. "You picked my clothes for me. The only people who have their outfits chosen for them are toddlers and dead people."

Kell laughed as she walked out. "That shirt looks good on you. The blue matches your eyes and the pink matches your cheeks when you get flustered. He'll love it."

"Flustered? What's that supposed—" I began, but she walked out and pulled the bedroom door closed.

"You've got like eight minutes," she hollered instead.

Shit. I hated to admit it, but the outfit she'd chosen was pretty good. I had considered wearing a yellow shirt, but this one was probably a safer option. Plus, he said he liked my Hawaiian-style shirts, and this one was flamingos and blue water. The skinny jeans were dark blue, and I opted for my white Converse.

When I went back into the bathroom to brush my teeth, Kell followed me in with a wine glass in her hand. She leaned against the counter and sipped her drink. "Who asked who?"

"He asked me," I said around my toothbrush.

"Eeeeeek!" She did a little wiggle. "How exciting! Do you know where you're going?"

"Dinner and the open-air cinema," I mumbled, then spat into the sink. "He said he thought *E.T.* was showing."

"Oh my God!" she let her head fall back with a groan. "That is so cool."

I brushed my hair. "It is, isn't it? As far as first dates go, I mean. Oh God, this is a first date."

"It's not scary, it's exciting," she said.

I shoved the deodorant can up under my shirt and sprayed my armpit. "Easy for you to say. You're here with your shoes off, drinking wine already." I sprayed the other armpit. "I'm about to endure the possibility of awkward silences and even more awkward questions. Oh my God, what if he likes football?"

She laughed and offered a shrug. "No one's perfect."

I looked her right in the eye, all jokes gone. "What if he doesn't like me?"

Her smiled faded. "Then he's not worth your time. And you can leave his arse there and come back here and drink wine and we'll watch *E.T.* because fuck anyone who doesn't like us." She raised her glass to that, then made a face. "Or, like we do most weekends, we can watch *Queer Eye* reruns and bawl our eyes out every episode."

I nodded. "Sounds like a plan."

She put her hand on my arm. "He'll like you just fine," she said warmly. "How can he not?"

"Thanks, Kell."

I splashed on some cologne and checked my phone. "Holy shit." It was 5:58. "I gotta go."

Kell followed me out. "Got keys, phone, wallet?"

I did the pocket check. "Yep."

"I won't wait up," she said with a wink.

With no time to overthink or panic-vomit, I was out the door. I dashed down the two flights of stairs into the street. It was a lovely spring night in Brisbane. The sun was getting low, the sky a perfect blue. It hadn't begun to get too humid yet, and a slight breeze teased the trees that lined the street.

It was kind of idyllic and I was going on a first date with Merrick, which was also idyllic, and he wasn't here yet, and then I realised I didn't know what kind of car he drove or even if he was coming at all. Should I have confirmed? Should I have tried to play it cool and been the one to be fashionably late?

Stop overthinking it, Leo. It's 6:01. He's not technically late yet. Well, one minute didn't constitute as lateness, did it? No, five or ten minutes is late. Actually half an hour is late. Five minutes is nothing. It's peak-hour traffic on a Friday, Leo. Give the guy a break.

"Jesus."

My phone buzzed with a message. *Turn around.*

I turned around and a small blue car parked up the street flashed its lights. The door opened and Merrick got out, smiling, and waved.

My grin said all that needed saying.

He wasn't late, he wasn't standing me up. Thank God.

"Hey," he said as I got closer.

"Hi."

"You good to go?"

"Sure."

"Hop in."

I got into the passenger seat and buckled up, and while he indicated, checked over his shoulder, and pulled the car out into the street, I took a moment to calm down.

"Were you waiting long?" I asked.

"Not at all," he replied. "I pulled into your street and there was a parking spot, so I grabbed it. I was just about to text you when I noticed you standing there. I didn't even see which building you came out of. You were beginning to look a little worried."

"I thought you might stand me up," I said stupidly.

"What? Why would I do that?"

"I don't know." It was obviously a reflection on me and my past experiences and not on him. "Sorry."

"You've been stood up before?"

"Once. It was horrible."

"That's awful!"

"I like to think he had some freak accident at the train station and ended up with amnesia and had no recollection of asking me." I sighed. "I could have been Sandra Bullock in *While You Were Sleeping*."

Merrick laughed. "Such a missed opportunity."

"I know!" I settled into the seat, all my nerves gone. "So how was your afternoon?"

"It was great. I even found some clothes without clay stains, so that's a bonus."

He wore olive green shorts and a white button-down shirt with the sleeves rolled to his elbows. A classic, smart-casual look. "You look great, by the way."

"Oh, thanks." A light pink coloured his cheeks. "I like your shirt. Flamingos are cool." He glanced at my thighs, enough to linger and appraise. "And the jeans."

Oh God. He just totally checked me out. And he said he liked me in skinny jeans. "Uh, well, you can thank Kell for that. I probably wouldn't have gone with the ultra-skinny jeans, but I was going to be late so she intervened."

His smile became a grin. "So I have Kell to thank for the ultra-skinny jeans and the double-tap on the Instagram photo that I thought was you so I messaged you, and long story short, here we are on a date."

"Ah, yep. Correct."

"Then I will thank her. For both."

Christ. I felt giddy. And I was certain I was six different shades of red. And I couldn't seem to speak, and I felt like I was floating. Was cloud nine really a thing? Because I thought I was on it.

"You okay?" he asked, still smiling.

"Oh yeah. I'm really fucking great, actually. How about you?"

He nodded and laughed. "Same."

Merrick found a parking spot along Brunswick Street, not far from the sprawling park where they were setting up the outdoor cinema. He popped the boot of his car and pulled out a basket. Like an actual picnic basket. "You came prepared," I said.

"Just a blanket and some water," he replied casually. "The food is here already."

Sure enough, there were several food trucks lined up for the moviegoers. There was a taco truck, a dumpling truck, a Thai noodles truck, and a Korean BBQ truck. There were hanging lights and lanterns, fairy lights, and I couldn't believe how amazing it all looked. "Oh my God. How have I never been here before? How long has this been going on?"

Merrick laughed. "It's only kinda new, I think? One of the ladies who takes my Monday class was telling me about it. She does community planning or something. Anyway, I thought it sounded pretty cool."

"It's amazing."

There was quite a crowd already and a lot of kids with parents, which was wonderful. Their excitement was contagious and I found myself smiling at some kids who were chasing each other.

After a moment, Merrick asked, "So, which truck do you think you want to get dinner from?"

"How about a little something from each truck and we can share?" I suggested, then realised some people hated sharing food. "Unless you'd rather just stick to your own thing. Do you have allergies or intolerances? I should have asked first."

He put his hand on my arm, his smile warm. "A little bit of everything sounds pretty good to me. And no, no allergies. I'd prefer no coriander though."

"Oh thank you, I can't stand that stuff either."

"It's an abomination." He grinned. "But I'm good with everything else, pretty much."

We selected a few things from each vendor and found a fairly decent spot in the park to watch the movie. Merrick took out the blanket and we set up our very own little picnic. It was ridiculous how happy I was, having a picnic in the park. We were far from alone, there were people everywhere, but on that blanket in the setting sun, it may as well have just been the two of us. It was romantic and sweet, and Merrick smelled so good and he was getting more good looking. His dark hair was neat and tidy, but his dark eyes were filled with light. We started on the dumplings first.

"Oh," I said, swallowing my first bite. "I almost forgot. Clyde scored your uncle's phone number."

Merrick's eyes popped wide. His smile became a grin. "Nooo, really?"

"Yes, really. Your uncle didn't tell you?"

"Of course he didn't." Merrick rolled his eyes, still smiling. "He never tells me anything. Especially about other men. God, I can't believe that. Are they going to meet up? A date, do you think?"

"I don't know. I hope so. From the second we walked in and Clyde laid eyes on him, he was a goner. I've never seen him at a loss for words before."

Merrick laughed. "I knew it! I knew they'd hit it off."

"You did. You suggested they meet." I finished my dumpling. "Unless that was just an excuse to call me."

He covered his mouth as he chewed and laughed at the same time. "No, really. I thought my uncle and Clyde would be good friends. One of my uncle's closest friends is a lot like Clyde. Kind of grumpy but loves to talk and would argue all day long, and my uncle loves the challenge. He told me once, nothing with his friend was ever boring. And when I met Clyde last week, he reminded me of my uncle's friend."

"Was there more to your uncle's friend than just a friend?"

"Not that I know of. But like I said, he wouldn't tell me. He's very quiet about his sexuality and would prefer the world just pretend everything's fine. He hated the idea of being an embarrassment to his family, and that made him unhappy for a long, long time."

"That's so sad."

Merrick nodded. "It is. He only ever talked to me about being gay after I came out. He came over to visit and I knew he wanted to say something but didn't know how. At first, I thought he was going to tell me being gay was wrong, but he told me he thought I was brave and how he wished his life had been different."

"Oh my God. That's awful. I'm so sorry."

Merrick gave me a sad smile. "Me too. But we became closer after that. I thanked him for being honest with me, and when he left that afternoon, he said he felt as though the weight of the world was off his shoulders. My mum, his sister, already knew, but he forbade her to talk about it. So he's kind of only open about anything with me."

His expression of pure joy in watching his uncle and Clyde talking in the studio made so much more sense now. "Well, I can see now why bringing him to the Bridge-the-Gap program was so important."

"It really was. And even if he and Clyde become friends and nothing more, it still worth it."

"Totally worth it. Though I now have to put up with Clyde boasting about scoring your uncle's phone number on their first meeting when I didn't get yours."

Merrick laughed, then deftly worked his chopsticks into the bowl of Hokkien noodles. "He's a harsh critic."

"The harshest." I sipped my water. "So tell me, how did you get into ceramics?"

"Uncle Donny taught me when I was a kid. He never took it seriously though; just a hobby. He used to do all kinds of craft, like needlepoint and macramé, though I never much cared for those. When I was about six or seven, during the school holidays when other kids were playing with LEGO, I was making little figurines and pinch pots, and I never grew out of it. I got my first potter's wheel when I was twelve."

"And you began your own business," I added. "That's awesome. And it's a great space. You have to be proud of that."

He stared at me for a long moment, his cheeks tinting pink and dark brown eyes intense. "I am. Thank you for saying that."

"Well, it's true. And I don't know much about business, but I know that can't have been easy."

He let out a breath. "No, it wasn't. But it's worth it." He rolled up a mini taco and bit into it, chewing thoughtfully. "It wasn't an easy decision, not at first. I was worried about costs and the debt and running a business, and the fear of failure almost stopped me. But my dad told me to believe in myself. Take a chance and to follow my heart. So I did."

That made me smile. "That's very good advice."

"It is," he said, meeting my gaze and not looking away. "It's something I'm working on in a personal capacity as well."

Oh shit. My heart thumped around in my chest. "And how's that going for you?"

"It's only kind of new," he answered with a cool smile. "I'll let you know tomorrow."

I barked out a laugh, turning bright red by the feel of my cheeks. "Right, then. No pressure."

He laughed and leaned back, resting on one elbow. "So tell me, what's the Leo Secombe story?"

"Very boring, really," I began. "I'm twenty-eight. Born and raised here in Brissy. My mum and dad split when I was four, but they still get on okay. I have an older sister, Brooke. She's married to Rob, who's a nice guy. They're talking about having a baby, which is great for them but drives me crazy. Did you want to guess how many conversations it takes about the importance of folate and fertility cycles and sex positions it takes for me to run away screaming? About seventy-six thousand. I don't know, that's probably an exaggeration. I lost count. But it's a lot."

He chuckled. "Duly noted."

"I mean, I'm happy for them, and I can't wait to be an uncle. But there are dots between my sister and sex that I don't ever need to join, thanks."

He laughed again, totally relaxed. "And you said you work retail?"

"Yeah, in the Queen Street Mall. I'm one of the store managers. It's not the worst job, but I work weekends, which is part and parcel of retail."

"I work weekends too," he said. "Our busiest two days."

"What days do you have off? Oh, do you have any days off? I guess being your own business makes it harder."

"Sometimes. If it's quiet, I'll take off for a bit. And I do try and separate myself from my work. Which isn't easy considering I also live above the studio."

"You do?"

"Yep. The upstairs loft is my home. It makes financial

sense, so I'm not paying rent on top of my studio lease. But having time away isn't easy. I usually go visiting family or friends when I need a time out." He finished his mini taco. "What days do you have off?"

"Fridays and Tuesdays. Fridays I spend with Clyde, usually. And Tuesday I get stuff done around the flat or go to the beach or catch up with a mate after they finish work."

"I love that you spend a day of the week with Clyde. It tells me a lot about what kind of person you are."

"Oh, thanks." I was glad it was getting dark so he couldn't see me blush. "And I love that you allowed a group of unruly seniors to do a class once a week."

He chuckled again. "I think it's a great program."

I finished my mouthful. "So, tell me about you, about your family."

"Well, I'm twenty-nine. I have two brothers. I'm the middle child, and yes, what they say about the middle-child syndrome is possibly true," he said with a smile. "It also probably explains why I spent so much time with my uncle growing up. My eldest brother is an accountant and my younger brother is a town planner; both successful, both married, both gave my parents grandkids." Then he paused and shot me a strange look. "I'm making it sound bad, aren't I?" he asked with a laugh. "My family and I are quite close, and me being gay never changed anything between us. I'm very lucky and I'm thankful for that. I mean, Uncle Donny's gay too, and no one ever had a problem with it, so it's all cool. But my mum still has a jibe every so often about how my brothers are professionals and how the grandkids are the apple of her eye. So she doesn't exactly say that my lack of university degree and children are a sore point, but it's something that hovers in the background."

"Oh, that's rough." I wanted to squeeze his hand but

didn't want to make it weird if he wasn't into public displays of affection, so I offered a frown instead. "I'm sorry to hear that."

"My dad and brothers and I have kind of made a bit of a joke out of it, so Mum's more aware of what she says now. So she is trying. My great, great grandfather on my mum's side was Japanese, so while my mum and uncle are very Australian in a lot of ways, they have those residual traditional expectations handed down from their grandparents. They were raised by their grandparents, basically, because their parents worked so much. That's just how it was."

"I get that."

He shook his head, more to himself than to me. "My great grandfather on my dad's side was from Argentina, so we have a real mix of strong traditions in my family." He made a face. "Sorry. Didn't mean to give you the whole Bowman family dynamics. We're not entirely as dysfunctional as I make us sound."

Not overthinking the public display of affection this time, I reached out and squeezed his hand. "Don't apologise."

He looked up at me, his eyes unreadable, before he sat up, keeping hold of my hand. He opened his mouth to say something, but the speakers crackled to life and the screen lit up as the movie began. So we packed up our food containers, sat side by side, and watched as the opening credits of *E.T.* began.

But just a few minutes into the film, he leaned a bit closer until our shoulders were touching. I glanced his way to find him smiling right at me before we both turned back to the screen. I ignored the butterflies in my belly and the warmth of his body, and how good he smelt, and made myself concentrate on the movie instead.

CHAPTER TEN

MERRICK

LEO SECOMBE WAS BRINGING me undone.

What was it about him that put me so off-balance? He was gorgeous, funny and quick-witted, smart and kind, and when I was with him, I was unguarded but completely comfortable. And to be frighteningly honest, I was dizzy with the *oomph* of it.

It was like some magical force, the thrill of new romance. And the possibility of where it might lead knocked me off my feet.

When he reached out and held my hand, just for a brief second, I thought my heart might stop. So when the movie began, we had our feet stretched out and leaned back on our hands, I shuffled in just a little closer so our shoulders touched, and then our arms, and about half an hour into the movie, his arm was under mine and our sides were almost completely touching.

He smelt divine. The heat of his body was electric.

I wasn't sure how much of the movie I saw. Leo laughed in all the right places so I could only assume he was watching and following the film. Me? I was lost to the rise and fall of his chest, how his side felt against mine, how his arm felt where it touched below my shoulder blade. All I could think about was the sound of his laughter and how I snuck glances at his profile in the dark. And did I mention how he smelt?

I wanted to know how he kissed and what he tasted like. I wanted to hold his hand properly and feel him against me. But it was more than just physical. I wanted to know about him, his past, his hopes for the future. I wanted . . . more.

Which was crazy, because this was date number one.

But he had me intrigued, that was for sure.

"You okay?" he asked quietly, snapping me out of my thoughts.

"Oh, sure." I checked the movie and it was almost over. "I was a million miles away."

"Thought it might have been too sad for you." He nudged into my side with a smile.

"Ah, no. Not *E.T.* If it was *Where the Red Fern Grows*, then yes."

He gasped. "Oh my God, I know, right? Kell and I bonded over that film and the level of sadness."

"It's cruel."

"That's what I said!"

I laughed, and we were so close, our faces just inches apart, and I could have so easily kissed him. Right then and there, I wanted to . . . but we hadn't discussed any kind of . . . *that* yet. But then he looked at my mouth and he licked his lips, and I almost died. God, I wanted to kiss him, and now his lips were wet and he leaned in, and I leaned in, my eyes fluttered closed, waiting—dying—for that contact.

The anticipation, the desire . . .

The round of applause as the movie ended scared the hell out of both of us. Everyone around us clapped and cheered, at the screen and not at us, thankfully. But Leo laughed nervously, his cheeks red and his bottom lip pulled in between his teeth.

Reluctantly, we applauded too, then huge lights came on and everyone began packing up. It was a shame, really, because it was such a beautiful night; I could have stayed there till morning. But we packed up our picnic and walked back to my car with a few dozen other people. Traffic was slow, gridlocked and unmoving for a bit, and I didn't want things to get awkward.

"I had the best night tonight," he said, beating me to it.

"Me too. Next month they're showing *The Wizard of Oz*, I think," I said. "Though next time we should bring pillows or something." I'd noticed a few other more prepared people were carrying some kind of pillow. "If you wanted to do this again, that is."

"Oh, those beanbag pillow things? Great idea. Though I'd probably fall asleep if I got too comfy. And yes, I'd love to do this again. Are you kidding me? The food was great, the movie was great, the company was . . ." He faked having to think about his word choice. "Above average."

I couldn't help but grin. "I'd really love to do this again too." Traffic began to move, so I had to concentrate for a bit as I made our way back to his place. "I assume I'm dropping you home, yeah? If you want to go out somewhere else . . ."

"No, home is fine. I need to be at work early tomorrow."

"Same."

"But thank you for asking. And thank you for picking me up and taking me home."

"You're welcome."

He looked at me for a moment before turning back to the passing city. "Yeah, my days of partying all night, then fronting up for work are well and truly behind me."

I laughed. "Yeah, same. Not that I ever really loved the clubbing scene. Maybe when I was first eighteen, but the shine of that wore off pretty quick. Not really my thing."

"Me either, to be honest. Kell and I usually do movie nights with pizza and a glass of wine, like the crazy party animals we are."

God, he made me laugh. "You and Kell sound pretty close."

"We are. She's like my sister. Her family were a bunch of arseholes to her when she came out, so she's part of my family now. Two years ago on her birthday, she tried to make peace with her parents and it didn't end well. They were still against her being lesbian, so we drank a shit load of wine and I adopted her. We had party hats and everything, and I made a very drunk certificate to make it official . . . Well, the certificate wasn't drunk. I was, and so was she. But we also had cake and she blew out some candles to seal the deal. It sounds kind of crazy, but after four bottles of wine at three o'clock in the morning, it made perfect sense to us."

I grinned at him. "You're a good friend . . . uh, brother, I mean."

"Thanks. I try to be."

I drove onto his street and slowed down. I didn't want this to be over just yet. I didn't want him to get out without a . . . what? A proper goodbye? Yeah. I had so much more I wanted to say. Or to ask, I guess. Luckily, there was a parking spot, so I pulled into it and cut the engine.

He sat there, not saying anything, or not opening his door. "So, this is me, I guess. That's my building there," he added, pointing to a white brick apartment block. He put his hand on the door. "I had a really good night, thank you."

I nodded. "Me too."

Christ. Did I lean over the console and kiss him? Did I ask first? Ugh. I hated this . . . My mouth was dry and my stomach was in knots. He opened the car door.

Think, Merrick. Say something.

"Well, have a good day at work tomorrow," he said, awkward and unsure. And then he got out.

I opened my door and shot out of my seat. "Leo, wait," I called out over the roof of my car.

He turned and smiled, and I let out a huge sigh of relief. "I don't know if I'm ready to say goodnight just yet," I blurted out. "I mean, I'm not inviting myself in. That's not what I meant. I just . . . I don't know."

He walked back over and leaned against the back door of my car. Was his blush from nerves or embarrassment? I wasn't sure. "I don't want to say goodnight just yet either."

I chuckled. "Thank God."

I shut my door and had to take this chance. This one last chance tonight to maybe kiss him . . . "Leo," I said quietly. I stepped in close, my feet on the outside of his. "I need to ask you something."

"Okay . . ." He frowned. "Sounds serious."

I laughed, pure nerves. "No . . . it's just . . . God. Can I kiss you?"

He nodded quickly. "Hell yes, you can. Please."

I chuckled, because clearly his nerves and excitement matched my own. I put my hand to his jaw and leaned in, watching his perfect face, his perfect lips part, his perfect eyes slowly close in that perfect moment before I kissed him.

The anticipation, the adrenaline, the thrill. I thought my heart might stop.

But his lips were soft and warm, his breath sweet. It was a tender kiss, a paradox to my thundering heart. And when that first kiss ended, I cupped his face and kissed him again. A little deeper with a hint of tongue, and he melted right into me.

There was no urgency, no hurried hands or push to take it further. Just a kiss. A perfect kiss.

We paused for breath when he smiled, and his eyes were a little unfocused. "Wow," he whispered.

"Yeah," I murmured. "Wow."

He chuckled. "Kinda glad I'm leaning against your car, or I'm sure I'd have fallen over." He laughed again. "My fucking knees are like jelly." I laughed with him and took a step back, but he pulled on my shirt. "Or you could stay right here."

"I could really stay right here," I said, kissing him again. I gave him more tongue this time, and he made a guttural sound that sent a jolt of something good right through me.

That sweet and tender kiss was now fast becoming something else.

"Fuck," I mumbled, out of breath, when I pulled my mouth away. My body was starting to react in ways Leo could no doubt feel.

He groaned and pulled my hips against his. *Yep, he could feel it.* "I was not going to ask you to come up," he said, his voice low. "Because I don't do that. Not on first dates. Not really on second dates, if I'm being honest. But right now . . ."

I laughed with relief and a kiss-drunk high. Because God, he was so right for me. "And I don't normally either, on second or even third dates. And if we were already in your apartment, I'm sure I would. But we should wait, yes?" I swallowed hard. "Waiting is good, right?"

He nodded, but he kept our bodies flush, pressed together. "Sure. Waiting is good." His tongue peeked out at the corner of his mouth, then his bottom lip disappeared between his teeth. "When will I see you again? Does that sound desperate? It probably does and I'm trying to decide if that bothers me."

I laughed again. "What are you doing tomorrow night?"

"Nothing," he whispered.

"Dinner? Say, seven thirty?"

He nodded. "Perfect."

"We'll go out somewhere, because maybe if we stay in . . ." I looked at his beautiful mouth.

"We won't be eating dinner," he finished for me.

I shook my head slowly. "Probably not." I inhaled deeply, trying to get my body under control. It didn't help that all I could smell was him. "I should probably go."

He gave the slightest of nods. "Or we could just say to hell with it. We both tried restraint. It was admirable. But I'm not convinced it's working out too well."

I burst out laughing and, this time, managed a proper step back. I took his hand and kissed his palm. "I don't want any regrets with you, Leo. I don't want you to have any regrets with me."

He gave me a grateful smile. "We can wait. Until tomorrow night or . . . whenever." Then, with a helluva lot more self-control than me, he kissed me quickly and took a few strides backward, toward his building. "Thank you, for the best first date ever."

"I'll text you tomorrow," I said, unable to stop from grinning.

He laughed and nodded, then shook his head like everything was crazy, and he turned and walked into the foyer of his apartment complex. I got into my car and let out a laugh, utterly stupefied.

Holy shit.

Just . . . wow.

I was more than giddy. I wanted to run and scream nonsensical words. I wanted to knock on his door and kiss him again. I wanted to take him out for dinner, I wanted to hold his hand, and I wanted to learn everything there was to know about Leo Secombe. I wanted to take him home tomorrow night and learn everything there was to know about Leo's body, in ways he never knew possible.

But first, I really needed to get home and take care of the painful hard-on that was demanding attention in my shorts.

"WHAT'S THE SMILE FOR?" Wesley asked. My brother had been eyeing me cautiously since he'd arrived early on Saturday morning.

Ciara laughed. "Yes, Merrick. What is that smile for?"

She had also been eyeing me since she arrived. She knew about my date with Leo, so she'd put two and two together, but I'd not divulged any details. Apparently I didn't need to. It was written all over my face. I pulled my lips into something that wasn't a smile. "No reason."

"Bullshit," Wesley said.

Ciara handed both of us our coffees. "He had a date last night. I think it's safe to assume it went well."

Wes shot me a look. "A date? You? On an actual date?"

"Oh shut it," I said, but I was smiling again. Or still. I didn't think I'd stopped smiling yet. "Yes. I went on a date. Yes, it went well. No, nothing happened." I gave them each a pointed look, landing on Wes last. "And no, you cannot say anything to Mum or Dad."

Wes laughed. "Like I'd put myself in that firing line."

"Exactly. I need to know if it's going to go anywhere first." I shrugged. "And if it does, then maybe after a few years, when we're happily married and possibly living in a different state, then I *might* mention to Mum that I'm seeing someone."

Wes snorted into his coffee. "Relatable."

"So you think you might marry him?" Ciara asked excitedly.

"I didn't mean that," I amended quickly.

"But you didn't say you wouldn't, either," she shot back, giving me one raised eyebrow.

I groaned. "He's great. Our date was great. But I'm trying not to read too much into it. I don't want to get ahead of myself. You both know it's been a while for me, so if you could ease up on the excitement . . ."

"Ah, brother," Wes said, putting his coffee down on the table. "Enjoy it. If it lasts a day or a week or a decade. Be excited if you want to be."

My heart did some ridiculous stuttering, skipping thing, and it drew a smile to my face. "He is kind of wonderful."

Ciara put her hands on my shoulders and gave me a gentle shake. "Ah! I'm so proud of you," she said in some singsong voice before going back to her café.

Wes kept his gaze cool, but he was fighting a smile. "It's true. This business has been your entire life for years. It'll be good for you to get out and get laid."

"Argh!" I put my hand up like a shield. "We don't need to have this conversation."

He laughed, then sipped his coffee. "So, you've got full classes again today?"

I nodded, thankful for the change in subject. "Yep. Full right through, nine till six."

"That's awesome."

"Oh," I said, just remembering. "Speaking of awesome. And this has to be a secret. You cannot tell a soul."

"Not even Em?"

Could he tell his wife? "No. No one."

His interest was piqued. He leaned in. "What is it?"

"I made Uncle Donny join in on a class yesterday."

His eyes narrowed. It obviously wasn't the gossip he wanted. "So?"

"It was a class for older LGBT folk, like a community support group."

His head tilted a little. "Oh?"

"Yep. And I might've kind of lined up a guy who I thought might be a good match," I said. "And there was an exchange of phone numbers, possibly a date."

His eyes went wide, his smile became a grin. "Noooo."

I nodded slowly. My grin matched his. "Yep. I got him to agree to an actual social event."

"Well, I'll be damned."

"You can't tell a soul. Uncle Donny doesn't know that I know. Promise me."

"Promise." He sipped his coffee, stunned. "Jeez, I don't come visit for one week and you both have dates!"

"Crazy, huh?"

"So tell me all about your guy," he said casually. "When are you seeing him next?."

"Tonight."

He stared at me. "You don't want to get ahead of yourself, but you're seeing him two nights in a row?" He laughed. "I'd say it's too late for that."

"I know." I shook my head and my younger brother just laughed some more. If I had any small objects handy that I could have thrown, I would have launched them at him. Instead, I aimed for something more mature. "Shut up."

CHAPTER ELEVEN

LEO

WORK WAS SO busy it passed in a blur, and on any other Saturday, I'd have gone home, planted my backside on the couch, and not moved until I dragged myself to bed. But this wasn't any other Saturday.

This was date number two with Merrick.

I hadn't slept much the night before. Given that I'd had to recount every detail for Kell, and given that my heart rate was well above normal and I was horny beyond belief, sleep hadn't come easy.

I had to take care of the very pressing issue inside my boxers because there was no way in hell it was going to go away on its own. And it wasn't just my dick that wanted release. It was my entire body. Merrick had set me on fire from my scalp to my toes.

And the way he kissed . . .

Holy shit, I wanted more of that.

I wanted to drown myself in it.

And tonight, all things going to plan, I intended to do just that.

"I still can't believe you both wanted it but both

declined," Kell said. "That's some pretty crazy self-control." She was ironing her dress in the lounge room.

"Yeah, well," I answered from my bedroom. "Self-control be damned tonight."

"Do you reckon you'll be coming back here tonight?"

I pulled on a shirt and walked out as I buttoned it up. "Why? Do you have similar plans?"

"If tonight goes well." She grinned at me and held up her dress. She was going out tonight with all the girls, and that included Selena, the woman Kell had had her eye on for some time. "Does this dress say eloquent with a dash of desperate?"

It was black, short, cinched in at all the right places, and low cut, and when she paired it with her leopard-print heels and red lipstick, she looked amazing. "More eloquent than desperate, but perfect. If Selena doesn't want you, she's blind. And possibly stupid."

Kell beamed at me. "Aww, thank you." Then she noticed my shirt. "Is that new?"

"I bought it today. You like?"

It had pale blue undertones with watercolour cherry blossoms. Still floral and still in keeping with my Hawaiian-esque shirt theme, but more subdued. "I love."

I half-turned and shot her a sultry look over my shoulder. "Does my outfit say to hell with eloquent, just give me a really good dicking?"

She laughed. "Perfectly."

"Good. Because that's the look I'm going for."

"Will you even make it through dinner?"

"I don't know. But I won't be disappointed if we don't."

She gave me the Katniss salute. "May the odds be ever in your favour."

I laughed and flattened down my jeans. "Seriously

though, do I look okay?" Now I'd finally had time to stop and think, the nerves were kicking in.

"You look amazing. Stop overthinking it, Leo. He totally likes you."

"God, I hope so."

Kell disappeared into her room and came out ten seconds later wearing the dress. "Did he tell you where he's taking you?"

"Nope. Not exactly. He just suggested a noodle bar not far from his place."

"What time is he picking you up?"

"Seven thirty." I checked my phone and let out a nervous breath. "Seven twenty-three."

She put her long hair up in an effortless ponytail, taming her blonde curls. "You've got everything taken care of: PrEP, lube, condoms?"

I nodded. Kell and I discussed all these things. "Yep. And you know you can call me at any time if you need, and I'll come get you, whatever the time. Stay together, be safe."

"Yes, Mum," she said affectionately.

"Have fun."

"I'd say the same to you, but it's a given." She kissed me on the cheek. "Go forth, my sweet child. Go get that dicking."

I laughed as I walked out, and I was still smiling when I got into Merrick's car. He'd pulled into the street as I got to the footpath, so I climbed straight in. "Hey," I said, trying not to notice how particularly gorgeous he looked tonight. He wore a navy button-down shirt and faded jeans, his short hair was glossy black, his smile, and his smell . . .

Jesus. I was ready to forego dinner and just get straight to the dicking.

"Hey," he replied huskily. He looked at me like he

might want to devour me. "You look so good."

Yep. Straight to the dicking. Please, and right now, thanks.

He let out a laugh as though he was nervous. "I told myself to try and play it cool. That didn't last very long."

"God, same."

He laughed again, but then his gaze darted to the rear-vision mirror. "Oh shit." There was a car behind us so he kept driving, and that was a good distraction. "How was work?"

"So busy. Actually, it was crazy-busy, but that was possibly a good thing because I was too busy to overthink everything and have a nervous breakdown before you picked me up. How about you?"

He grinned at me. "About the same."

The electricity between us was insane. I was surprised there weren't actual physical sparks. My heart was doing some squeezy-hammering thing; I couldn't seem to breathe properly, my skin was warm all over, and all I wanted to do was laugh. "Ooooh boy," I said, trying to catch my breath, grinning like an idiot. "So where are we going for dinner?"

"It's an Asian-fusion noodle bar," he answered. "They have everything. You hungry?"

"I am, actually. I didn't really get a lunch break."

"Well, the food at this place is amazing." He looked down at my shirt again before meeting my eyes. "I really like that shirt."

I almost said *where I would like to see it end up* but decided against it. "Uh, thanks."

He shot me an odd look. "What's so funny?"

"Nothing." I was still grinning, and I figured what the hell. "I was just thinking . . . if you really like my shirt, I'll be only too happy to leave it on your bedroom floor tonight."

He burst out laughing, surprised but amused. "Is that so?"

"Yeah, sorry. Corny pickup lines are terrible."

"Not completely terrible. I liked where that one was going."

He pulled the car into a parking spot and I realised then where we were. We were at his studio, or more significantly, at his house. "Oh. Was the offer of my shirt on your bedroom floor better than dinner? Because seriously, I won't mind."

He laughed again and got out of the car. "I'd be lying if I said it wasn't." He nodded up the street. "But the restaurant is within walking distance."

We got out of the car, and I kind of felt bad that he had come to pick me up only to drive straight back to his house. "I could have driven to your place," I said.

He put his hands to his heart. "But it's a date. My dad always said I had to date properly. Pick them up, drop them home. Be a gentleman, that kind of thing."

"Pretty sure your dad was just looking after your virtue. By picking your date up and then dropping them home, you'd be minimising the time spent at your place."

Merrick laughed. "Maybe."

I looked at the studio, at the darkened windows, at the privacy. And my empty stomach was forgotten, because inside that ceramics studio—or rather, in the loft above it—was privacy for kissing, touching, tasting . . .

I pointed my thumb towards the front door with the closed sign. "If you'd like to take me upstairs right now, I could help you find that virtue . . ."

Merrick barked at a laugh and grabbed my hand. "Dinner first. Conversations and questions. Then we can worry about virtues."

As we walked up the street, Merrick kept a hold of my hand. I threaded our fingers properly, and the adrenaline and the nerves, the anticipation, and the sexual tension manifested as a shit-eating grin.

The restaurant was only a block away, but there wasn't just one place to eat. There were heaps on both sides of the street. I could see lots of people, smiling and eating, seated at tables inside each one. "Man, I wish Kell and I had a dozen different restaurants a block away."

"Perks of living in a semi-commercial zoned part of the city," Merrick said as he held the door open for me. "Means I don't have to cook very often."

It was busy inside, but thankfully Merrick had made a reservation. We were shown to our table by a woman who knew Merrick by name, and we each ordered a Coke. "You *do* come here often."

He nodded. "The *japchae* is to die for. And the *shoyu* ramen is better than my grandmother's, but if anyone else asks, I'll deny I ever said that."

I chuckled and sipped my drink. As much as I had wanted Merrick to take me upstairs at his studio, I was really glad he had opted for dinner first. He was right; there would be time for that later. Getting to know each other and being certain that this thing between us was right was too important to ignore.

"So," I began, "you wanted conversations and questions . . . What did you want to ask?"

"Everything," he replied simply. "I want to know everything."

God, that could be dangerous. "Such as?"

"Favourite colour?"

I snorted, because that was not what I expect him to ask. "Um, it depends. Are we talking about Skittles? Or having to choose one colour to wear for the rest of your life? Because they have vastly different selection criteria."

My answer clearly surprised him. He almost choked on his drink. "Okay, sorry. I should have been more specific. Favourite colour Skittle?"

"The purple ones, of course."

"Of course."

"Yours?"

"Orange."

"Least favourite?"

"Yellow."

"No one eats the yellow Skittles."

He grinned. "Favourite colour M&M's?"

"The normal ones or the peanut ones?"

"Both. Either."

"I prefer the peanut ones, not gonna lie. Blue ones are my favourite. Yours?"

"I like the normal M&M's better, and I eat the brown ones first. The red ones die last, and all other colours are indiscriminately picked off at random."

"Ooh, organised chaos. I like that."

Merrick laughed again. "And if you had to choose a colour to wear every day for the rest of your life?"

"Probably blue. It's more adaptable for more situations. I love splashes of pink, but wearing it head to toe every day of forever would be a bit overwhelming."

"Agreed. Very Umbridge."

Now it was me who laughed. "God, I didn't even think of that. She was so evil."

The waitress came back and took our order, but because we hadn't even looked at the menu, Merrick ordered for the both of us. I figured it'd be interesting to see what he chose, what he thought I'd like.

"Okay, my turn to ask a question. Dating history. And go . . ."

He made a face. "Wow, okay. You just jump right in."

"Well, we have discussed Skittles and M&M's, so there's nowhere left to go, really."

He chuckled again. "This is true. But honestly, there's not much to tell. My work and the business have been one hundred per cent of my time for the last four years. Well, five years if you count the planning. Which sounds really sad, and it's not, really. It wasn't really a choice. I was just . . . busy. Seven days a week, night and day. I mean, there were a few guys over the years . . . but nothing serious and nothing more than once." He cleared his throat. "That sounds bad, sorry. But before that, I had a long-term boyfriend. We were together for four years but we weren't what we wanted. It was my split with him, ultimately, that gave me the push to open the studio. You know, that whole 'what do I really want to do with my life' moment type of thing." He sighed and gave me half a smile. "Like I said. Pretty boring. What about you?"

"My dating history? There's not much to tell. I've had two serious boyfriends in my life. The first straight out of high school, the second when I was twenty-three. Both lasted about two years, no tragic ending, we'd just run our course. And for the last few years, I either hang out with Kell or with Clyde. I also have split days off and I work weekends, which makes it hard to spend time with some-one. Know what I mean?"

"Absolutely. I know exactly what you mean. You need to find someone who also works weekends who might be able to score coinciding days off."

I blushed. "I'm working on that, actually."

"Oh, lucky him."

"Lucky me."

His smile twisted thoughtfully, his dark eyes met mine, and I knew whatever he was about to say would be intense. "A hypothetical question. If you were to, say, come over to my place tonight and found that I only have bunk beds, would you prefer the top or the bottom?"

Oooh boy. His question made me feel warm all over, my belly tightened, my heart squeezed. *Top or bottom?* Did he really have to ask? I mean, it wasn't polite to assume anything, but he gave off top-vibes. Maybe my outfit didn't say 'please dick me' as much as I thought. My nerves escaped me in a laugh. "One hundred per cent the bottom bunk. Never was a fan of being on the top bunk, so yeah, the bottom bunk. Very, very thoroughly."

Merrick squirmed in his seat and cleared his throat. "I'm very, very thoroughly glad you said that." He pulled at his collar. "Is it hot in here?"

"A little." I took a breath and tried to calm my heart rate before it tapped out on me. "So, uh . . . Hypothetically, do you have bunk beds?"

He shook his head with a laugh. "No."

"I'm also thoroughly glad to hear that."

"There's a lot of thoroughlies."

"I'm hoping there's more later on." I sipped my drink and watched as he tried to school his expression.

"Jesus." His cheeks were flushed pink, his eyes were onyx, and his tongue peeked out to wet the corner of his mouth. Then he glanced around the room. "Christ, where is our food?"

And right on cue, the waitress appeared with two plates. One was a noodle dish that I couldn't remember the name of, and the other was steamed dumplings and different dipping sauces. It all smelt delicious.

I picked up my chopsticks and decided that we should try a conversation that didn't flounder into the waters of sexual innuendo. "So, a non-hypothetical question," I began as I selected a dumpling. "Why ceramics? What is it about working with clay that you love?"

He finished dishing out some noodles from the share plate into his smaller bowl. He seemed to consider his answer. "I love how it can be shaped into practical, usable things. I love how it can become something else. The art of clay has been around for thousands of years, from almost every different ancient culture in some way, and I love that it connects us."

I stared at him. "Wow."

He blushed again and let out a nervous laugh. "I love how it feels," he continued. "It's familiar and comforting, and it relaxes me. Sitting at my wheel, throwing clay, it's a simple joy for me. And the firing process always excites me. You just never really know what you're going to get. I can use different textures and add different firing elements like wood or foil, copper or leaves, and it's always something different." He gave me a bright smile. "And it involves all the elements. Water, earth, air, and fire. There's something about that that speaks to me."

I couldn't believe what he was saying. Not what he said, exactly, but how he said it. The unapologetic passion he had. "I'm jealous," I admitted, then realised how that sounded. "Not of the clay. Well, maybe a little. But that you have something you're so passionate about."

"You don't?"

"Not really. Not like that."

"Perhaps you haven't found it yet."

"I hope so. I mean, I'd like to."

He took another mouthful and chewed thoughtfully

before swallowing. "What did you want to be when you were younger?"

"Rapunzel."

He laughed. "And how's that working out for you?"

I ruffled my hair. "Could never stand to grow my hair long, which was kind of critical to the role."

He smiled around a mouthful of dumpling. "Kind of, yeah. Albeit discriminatory for the follicly challenged."

"That's very true. And waiting for my Prince Charming was a bust."

"Not to mention unrealistic."

"Grossly unrealistic. Not all princesses need rescuing."

Merrick grinned. "And not all princes are the heroes."

"And they certainly don't all ride in on their trusty steeds from their faraway castles," I added. "Sometimes they drive a Ford Focus and own a ceramics store."

Now he laughed. "Are you knocking my car?"

"Not at all. In fact, if Disney were to adapt their princess classics to the twenty-first century, the trusty white steed would definitely now be a blue Ford Focus."

"And their princesses could be boys with short hair if they so wished."

"Hell yes."

Merrick stared at me for a long few seconds. There was nothing but kindness and subtle amusement in his eyes. We ate in silence for a bit, until I threw my serviette over my plate in defeat. Merrick took in one more mouthful, then did the same. "How was your food?"

We'd eaten most of what had been put between us. "Perfect. Have you had enough?"

He nodded. "Yep."

Which meant it was time to leave . . . which meant it was time to go back to Merrick's place . . .

Nerves fluttered low in my belly. We halved the bill and went outside into the cool Brisbane night. There was a gentle breeze, and laughter rang from one of the restaurants, and the street had a pleasant hipster vibe, though it darkened somewhat toward Merrick's place. "It must be pretty cool living so central. You can just walk everywhere."

"The restaurants and coffee shops are kind of new. They began to sprout up after I bought my studio, which is great for business." Merrick slipped his hand into mine, lacing our fingers. "Is this okay?" he asked. "Some people don't care much for it."

I gave his fingers a squeeze. "It's more than okay with me." And it was. It had been years since I'd held hands with someone, and it gave me a thrill to do it now. "I like it."

"Me too," he replied.

His studio came into view, and my nerves ratcheted up a notch or three. All that talk, the anticipation, was about to become reality. When we stopped at the front door to the studio, Merrick grabbed the keys from his pocket, took one look at my face, and stopped. "You okay?"

"Nervous."

"You are?" He didn't seem to believe me. "You were all talk before. Like you wanted this. We certainly don't have to—"

"I want to," I blurted out. "Just nervous about it, that's all. In a good way. You know, anticipation. And all the talk before was easy. Now I have expectations to worry about."

He smiled. "Yours or mine?"

"Your expectations of me."

"Do you overthink things often?"

"All the time."

Merrick unlocked the door and stepped inside. He punched in a security code, then held the door open for me.

The small café area was familiar, even in the dark. Once the doors were locked again, Merrick took my hand and led me to the long work table in the studio where we'd sat making our pinch pots.

When my arse was against the table, I sat on it and he stood between my legs. "Before we go upstairs, I want you to know we don't have to do anything. We can just talk or just kiss. There's no pressure to do anything else. We don't even have to go upstairs if you don't want. I can drive you home any time."

"I want to."

"But?"

"There's no but. I just overthink things, and it's been a while for me, so I was just a little nervous."

Merrick's lips twisted and he sighed. "Can I suggest something?"

"Sure."

"How about we wait?"

"Wait for what?"

He made a face. "Before we have sex."

"Um, okay."

"You don't sound convinced."

"Don't think you need to do this on my behalf. I know we both said we'd like to wait, like a third date or whatever, but, well, now I don't know . . ."

"Leo, I just don't want to rush this." He swallowed hard. "Is that weird?"

"Not at all," I said, shaking my head. "I don't want you to do anything you're not comfortable doing."

"I'm fine with doing . . . other things. Other sexual things, but just not . . . penetrative sex. I just prefer to know the guy first, and I don't want to rush this."

"What kind of sexual things?"

Merrick chuckled. "Well, I'm fond of orgasms."

I snorted, because that was not what I had expected him to say. "What a coincidence. So am I!"

He chuckled again, but his eyes were warm. "I'm comfortable with doing naked things. But I've done the one-nighters, Leo. And I don't want that with you."

"Oh."

He rubbed his thumb over my cheek. "I want more than just one night."

"Me too."

"For me," he explained, "being inside someone is personal and profound. I want that connection. I know a lot of guys don't agree with that. It's all sex, and I get that. It is. But for me, some things mean more than others. And I want that connection with you. I want it to mean something more." He swallowed hard. "And I guess the fact I'm even telling you this already tells me that I like you, Leo. Because if I didn't, I wouldn't care what we did."

"I like you too," I whispered, grateful for the lack of lighting so he couldn't see me blush. "And I get it. I do."

"So should we establish some boundaries?"

"Sure."

"Naked orgasms," he said again. "Hand jobs, blow jobs, that kind of thing."

I swallowed hard, and my heart almost expired. "Oh, sure," I squeaked. "I like those things."

Merrick's smile was warm, and he was so close, his warmth, his smell was intoxicating. "Are you sure?"

"One thousand per cent. I'm pretty sure if you just even kissed me right now, it would be enough."

So he kissed me. He was gentle at first, with a soft press of his lips, and he tilted my chin up. I opened my mouth for him and he rewarded me with his tongue, sending a flash of heat through my body. Then, with confident hands, he pulled my arse closer to the edge of the table so I could feel his erection.

I groaned like I was starring in a B-Grade porn film, and I couldn't even be embarrassed because it spurred him on. He kissed me deeper, held me tighter, and my God, we weren't even going to make it up the stairs. We were going to dry hump down here on his studio work table . . .

He seemed to realise this at the same time as me, because he pulled his mouth from mine. He was panting, his lips swollen. "How's the overthinking?"

"The what?" I asked. "I've got nothing . . . My brain . . . Nope. Just you." I swallowed hard, trying to get my brain to work. "What I meant to say is, you really need to take me upstairs."

Merrick laughed and, taking my hand, pulled me to my feet before he led me to the cast iron stairs, and I followed him up. The only light came from a table lamp and from a street light outside, so I could see the general layout sans the finer details.

I had no idea what to expect, and yes, he'd called it a loft. But it was more than that. It had high ceilings and exposed rafters. Like the studio downstairs, the walls were white with the exposed black pipes that ran like lonely highways up the walls. The space itself was completely open. There were no walls separating anything, and it was L-shaped. The entry opened into the lounge area with a sofa and a TV, which flowed into a kitchen and dining area in the corner, and around the L-turn was the bedroom. "Bathroom's in there," he whispered, nodding to the wall behind his bedhead. He still had my hand in his, and I was reluctant to let it go.

I couldn't take my eyes off the bed. He took my chin

between his thumb and forefinger. "Tell me where you want me to start?"

What my body wanted—though I wouldn't say this out loud—was a thorough dicking, and it had wanted it for hours and hours. But my heart wanted more than just that too. I didn't want dicking to be the end-all of our sexual experiences. I wanted to build to that. "I want everything. But first, I want to know your body, and I want you to learn mine. I want to become familiar with your touch, and I want to know what you taste like."

He closed his eyes and his nostrils flared. "Jesus, Leo. You're gonna finish me before you even touch me."

"Well, thank God I didn't just come right out and say I want you buried inside me for hours in the most thorough dicking, ever."

He stared, then blinked before he burst out laughing. He kissed me with smiling lips. "Another time, perhaps."

I nodded. "Yes, please."

He shivered, and his smile faded, his gaze bore into mine. "I need you naked." He undid my shirt buttons and slid the fabric over my shoulders until it fell behind me. "Oh yeah," he murmured, caressing a finger over the hair on my chest, and he planted a kiss on my collarbone. He drew his nose up my neck at the same time he pulled the button on my jeans, tugging my body against his, our hardened cocks pressed between us as he gave me a filthy kiss.

Oh, hell yes.

He was just the right mix of tender and demanding, and I fucking loved it. I was putty in his hands . . . or rather, I was clay in his hands. I toed out of my shoes and fumbled out of my jeans until I stood completely naked in front of him.

"Oh wow," he murmured. He appraised me, his gaze

raking over me as though I was simply the most delectable thing he'd ever seen. He licked his lips and hummed as he ran his hands over my chest, down my belly to my cock. He wrapped his hand around me, and I think I whimpered.

"You're very overdressed," I whispered, making a start on his shirt. I only got the first few buttons undone before I lifted the hem and pulled it over his head. I palmed his rock-hard cock through his jeans, earning a hiss from him before I popped the button and pushed his jeans and briefs down. He kicked off his shoes and shucked out of his pants. His body was lean, far more muscular than his shirts suggested. He had defined biceps and forearms, his hands were smooth and gentle, and a dark line of hair ran from his navel to where his gorgeous cock stood out proudly.

"Get on the bed," he said, his voice like velvet.

I did as he asked, then he did as I had asked. He learned my body, studying every inch of skin with his mouth and eager hands. He touched, skimmed, massaged, pulled, and pumped. He licked and sucked and kissed, and my entire body felt as if it were on fire. Alight with pleasure and desire, and I was so close. So very close.

"Your turn," I said, rolling us over. He went willingly, happily, spreading his legs and rolling his hips. I kissed him long and hard, tasting his delicious mouth and that delectable tongue. He groaned and held my face as we kissed, as though he couldn't get enough of me.

It was a heady feeling.

I wanted to do to his body what he'd done to mine. I wanted him to beg me, I wanted his whole body to sing. I kissed down his jaw, his neck, which he very obviously loved. I sucked on his nipples, and his chuckle became a moan. I kissed his belly, his hip, and licked a stripe up the length of his dick, tonguing the glans and the slit.

He gripped his bedding. "God, Leo. I'm not gonna last."

I squeezed the base of his shaft to stem his orgasm and he groaned, but then I sucked on the head and brought him right back to the brink. I pulled off, savouring the taste of him. "You taste so good."

"Oh fuck," he rasped, like this pleasure bordered on pain.

I was too turned on to drag it out, and his cock was so swollen, I knew he was close. So I crawled back up his body, aligning our cocks and taking both in my hand. I swallowed his groan with a hard kiss and he bucked up into my fist as he came.

Hot pulses of come splashed between us as he cried out, and I followed right after him.

My orgasm rocketed through me, blinding heat and liquid fire, and I came on his belly and chest. The room spun and I lost all sight and sound, everything but Merrick's arms holding me, his mouth whispering against mine. "Oh fuck, yes."

I collapsed on top of him and I worried for a split second about the mess smeared between us, but Merrick's arms tightened around me, his mouth on my neck and at my ear. He kissed and whispered the sweetest nothings until our breathing returned to normal.

"You okay?" he whispered.

"I think I died," I mumbled. I leaned back so I could see his beautiful eyes. "Actually, I think I might have just had an out-of-body experience."

He smirked up at me, scanning my face. And for a horrible second, I thought it was about to get weird. Or that he would kick me out and never want to see me again. But then he lightly brushed my hair off my forehead. "I want you to stay."

CHAPTER TWELVE

MERRICK

"STAY," I repeated. "Shower with me and spend the night in my bed."

Leo blinked and a slow smile pulled at his lips. "Are you sure?"

"Yes. I want round two tonight, and I want to wake up next to you and possibly go for round three."

"Are you bribing me with orgasms?"

"That depends. Are you okay with that?"

"Uh, hell yes."

"Then yes, I'm bribing you with orgasms."

"I work tomorrow at nine."

"I'll drive you."

He laughed. "Consider me bribed."

I rolled us over and peeled myself from him, considering we were glued together. It felt gross, but I'd be lying if I said I didn't like it. Having his come on my skin and mine on his was a weirdly sexy thing. And yeah, I knew it was some primal crap, but I didn't care. The smell of sex was potent and intoxicating, and I wanted more.

I wanted him to stay. I wanted him to sleep in my bed. I

wanted my bed to smell of him, and I wanted to hold him and kiss him all night.

I'd forgotten how wonderful kissing was. I'd forgotten how healing it was to be held by someone. And it was probably far too soon to invite him to stay, but to hell with societal expectations.

This felt right.

I led Leo to my bathroom and flipped on the lights. "Oh wow," he said.

"Yeah, the lights are a bit bright, sorry."

"No, not the lights. Your bathroom is awesome."

"Oh." I chuckled. "It used to be the utility room when this was a warehouse. It's pretty cool, huh?"

The room was big for a bathroom, with white subway tiles and two opaque windows. There was enough room for a walk-in shower, toilet, huge vanity cupboard, but also enough space for a washing machine and dryer and a built-in linen press. I grabbed two clean towels and hung them at the end of the shower cubicle and started the water. "Downside is the hot water isn't exactly fast. It takes a few seconds to kick in."

And even though I'd just explored his body, only now did I get to see it with proper lighting. Leo was so handsome, and his body was impeccable. He wasn't a twink, exactly, and he wasn't all buffed up like a gym junkie. He had a spattering of hair on his chest, which I immediately ran my fingers through again, and his cock hung heavy. He was circumcised, and he didn't shave or wax anywhere, and he wasn't like the guys who preened about their bodies. It was refreshing and exciting, and I couldn't take my eyes off him.

He was just perfectly normal. And fucking gorgeous.

"You're staring at me," he said. Then he looked at his chest, then mine. "Is it our jizz?"

"Christ, you're gonna get me hard again," I mumbled, and sure enough, my cock visibly twitched, which he most definitely saw, and I gave it a squeezy-stroke. "It's you. I'm very attracted to you, but yes, being covered in our jizz doesn't help."

He laughed. "You're attracted to me?"

"God, yes." I checked the water temperature and stepped in under the spray. "You sound surprised."

"Well, I am, I guess," he replied.

I squirted the body puff with the shower gel and soaped up my belly and chest and gave my dick and balls a scrub too. When I looked up, he was still outside the shower, staring at me. "You okay?" I asked.

"Oh, sure." He shook his head a little and stepped into the shower with me. "I was just appreciating the view."

I traded places with him and washed him over with the soapy puff. Only when he rinsed off and tilted his head back, my gaze was drawn to the column of his throat. His neck and the vein that protruded there . . . When he brought his head forward out of the water, I held his face and captured his mouth with mine.

God, he was so sexy. I never wanted to stop. I wanted this thrill to last forever.

My dick began to thicken again, and he moaned when it pressed between us. "Oh Christ," he gasped, grinding against me. It made my head spin and my knees weak.

"We should," I panted. He kissed my neck and explored my body with frantic hands and an eager mouth. "Go back to . . . oh God . . . back to bed."

He nodded against my jaw, and I somehow managed to shut the water off. I handed him a towel and managed to dry myself off in record time. I was fully hard again, my balls so heavy with desire I doubted we'd be sleeping much tonight. Penetrative sex, no. I wasn't ready for that. But everything else, yes . . .

Leo scrubbed the towel over his hair, and his gaze fell to my erection, then drew back up to my eyes. His jaw was slack, his eyes dark with want, the towel forgotten. "I need that."

"Need or want?"

"Need. And want, but mostly need." He groaned and his cock jerked, almost fully erect. He put his hand to his forehead and looked a little pained.

"What's wrong?" I asked.

"I'm trying really hard not to ask you to fuck me. But we're doing the holding-out thing, right?"

I chuckled and lifted his knuckles up to my lips. "Do you not think it will be worth the wait?"

"Never did have much patience."

"Believe me. I'm right there with you. I want it too."

"Then why don't we?"

I kissed his palm, his wrist. "I don't want to risk rushing this. I don't want to risk . . . us. We barely know each other and I want more than that with you. Hand jobs and blow jobs are one thing, but sex, intercourse, that's something else for me. I want . . . I really want to see where we can go. And I'm pretty sure if we start fucking, we'll miss something. I don't want to fizzle out because we burned too hot, too soon. Does that make sense?"

He pouted but conceded a nod. "It does. It just feels a little like . . . rejection."

I cupped his jaw and met his gaze with an intense stare. "It's not rejection, Leo. Believe me. I want you. I want you in my bed. I want to be inside you. I want to give you that, and God, I want to take it." His nostrils flared and I kissed him gently, then whispered against his lips, "I'm not rejecting you. If you really want it, Leo, we can."

He smiled now, though he kept his eyes closed. "No, you're right, sorry. I shouldn't have pushed. You put down boundaries and I respect that. I get that. My heart knows that, and my brain knows that. But my dick . . ."

I reached down and took said dick in my hand and gave him a long, slow stroke. "How about I suck it until it feels better."

He laughed and I took his hand this time and led him back to my bed. "Lie down," I instructed. I followed him onto the mattress and instead of lavishing attention all over his body, I went straight to the prize. I took him into my mouth and pumped his shaft, hard and fast, and he was a writhing, groaning mess of incoherent words by the time he came down my throat.

He lay dazed and smiling as I kissed my way up his body. I lifted one of his eyelids. "You alive in there?"

He laughed. "You don't play fair."

"I never said I did."

His eyes were dreamy, his smile lazy and cute, and when he shifted his leg, it brushed my still-hard cock. "Mmm." He licked his lips. "I'm too boneless. You're gonna have to bring it up here."

"Like home delivery."

He chuckled. "You're getting a five-star Uber Eats rating. Just so you know."

I burst out laughing, planting a kiss on his mouth before crawling further up the bed. I held onto the bedhead and straddled his chest. He wiggled down a bit more and took me into his mouth.

Oh God.

I rocked in slowly. His lips closed around me. His flattened tongue worked me over with each thrust. The slick warmth, wet and divine, felt so damn good. I tried not to go too deep, but he gripped my arse and sucked me in.

All the fucking way.

My orgasm came without warning, like a bomb dropped from the stratosphere, nuking everything in its path. Leo only released me so I could collapse on the bed. We were a mess of tangled limbs and sated smiles, the room was spinning, or maybe it was just my mind.

He pulled me into his arms and anchored me with a kiss to my forehead. "Goodnight, Merrick."

CHAPTER THIRTEEN

LEO

AS SOON AS I got through the door after work on Sunday, Kell pounced on me. "Oh my God, tell me everything."

I laughed because I'd expected that exact reaction. "It was . . . great."

She tilted her head. "Uh-oh."

I dumped my keys and wallet on the kitchen counter. "Uh-oh, what?"

"You don't sound very convincing." She went to the fridge, took out the wine, and poured two glasses. She handed me one. "Tell me everything."

I sighed. "I'm just . . . last night was great. It was amazing."

"Was there dicking?"

I made a face. "Kind of . . . We did . . . stuff. Twice last night and again this morning in the shower before he drove me to work."

She stopped, her wine almost to her lips, and blinked. "Three times?"

I laughed.

She stared. "Three times, and you're not happy? Christ almighty, Leo. Your expectation settings are aimed just a smidge too high. Or completely broken. I'm gonna just go with broken."

"I know." I sipped the wine and sighed. "Thank you for this. Work sucked today."

"Oh, Leo." She frowned. "What's really the matter?"

"I don't know . . . it's just . . . he's so perfect. He's smart and charming and funny, and he's gorgeous."

"So what's the problem?"

"He wouldn't have sex with me." I groaned because I sounded so petty. "I sound like a whiny bitch, I know. But I asked him to, which was probably closer to begging than asking, and he said no."

"He said no?"

"We'd already got through round one, and . . ." Then I corrected. "Actually, the sexual tension between us was so high we almost didn't even go to dinner. But we did because we're grown-ups. We made it back to his place. I was nervous, and he was so cool, calm, and collected. He told me we didn't have to do anything and that we should probably wait before fucking. But he said other things were cool. I told him I was happy with other things. And we did, and holy hell, it was good. *He's* good. Now I don't know if he has a master's degree in pleasuring the human male anatomy, but he should have. I would give him an honorary doctorate, if you get my drift."

Kell laughed. "Okay, so that all sounds good so far."

"It was. We get into the shower, and things get real hot, real quick again. Like God, Kell. He just does something to me. I can't even explain it. So I basically say, 'I know we're trying to hold out, but could you pretty please fuck me into next week like right now, thanks?' and he said no."

Kell put her wine down, her eyebrows knitted in confusion. "Wait, stop, back up. You agreed to hold out? Like you're going to wait for a bit?"

I downed a mouthful of wine. "Yes. Well, he did, and I agreed. He wants to wait. Doing other things is fine, but no fucking. He needs a deeper connection and doesn't want us to fizzle out. And I *did* agree, but then I wanted it."

She took a second to process all this, then gave me a sad smile. "Leo, honey, you know I love you . . ."

I groaned. "I know, I know. He's right, and I'm being a selfish, sex-crazed idiot." I put my face in my hands. "He must think I'm so desperate."

Kell put her hand on my shoulder. "There's nothing wrong with wanting something. And voicing that you want something."

I sagged. "I told him I felt a bit rejected because he turned me down. Like who the fuck says that?"

"Well-adjusted, socially empathetic grown-arse men, that's who." She gave me a toast with her wine glass. "Your therapist would be proud. If you had one."

"You're my therapist," I said, then added, "Best friend slash flatmate slash therapist."

"Then I'm proud."

"Why do I feel so bad?"

"Because you wanted a dicking."

I sighed. "I did."

"He did wring one out of you three times though. That's a fucking big fat kudos to him right there, let me tell you."

"How much wine have you had?"

"Half a bottle."

I laughed and clinked my glass to hers. "How was your night?"

Kell grinned. "Selena left at lunchtime."

My mouth fell open. "No way!"

"Yes way. Best sex of my life."

"It was the dress. Told you she'd love it."

"Maybe it was the dress. Or it could have been me arguing that Carol Danvers would totally beat Diana Prince's arse."

I snorted. "That would do it."

"And the fact I finally scrounged up enough courage to tell her I thought she was gorgeous, and apparently she'd been crushing on me for months too but didn't want to make it awkward."

"Oh, so *you* speak up and get the best sex of your life, and *I* speak up and get . . ." I reconsidered. "Okay, so three times is pretty good. And his hands . . . like, holy shit. He's a ceramicist, right. So he *knows* how to use his hands. And his arms, and his mouth, oh my God."

"And he wants to wait, Leo," Kell said gently.

"So we don't burn too bright and fizzle out was how he explained it."

"That means he likes you."

I nodded. "He said he did. He said he wanted more with me and to see where we might go."

Kell's eyes softened and she put her hand to her mouth. "Oh, Leo. He really does like you. He really does."

"Okay, Sally Field. You've had enough wine."

She snorted and clinked her glass to mine again. "I need a refill and pizza for dinner."

Pizza actually sounded great. "I'll order it."

"When are you seeing Merrick again?"

I took my phone out, about to open the Domino's app. "I'm not sure. He said he'd text me. He had work today as well, then some family dinner thing." I stared from my phone to Kell. "Oh God. What if he thinks I'm some desperate-for-a-dicking slut-man and doesn't want to see me again because he put down consent-boundaries and I tried to talk him out of it. Oh God, I tried to talk him out of his consent-boundaries." I could feel a meltdown coming on . . .

"Leopold Curtis Secombe," she said sternly. "Don't start that shit. Send him a quick text right now, thanking him for a great night."

"My name is not Leopold, as you're very well aware. And where the hell did the Curtis come from?"

"When I need to full name you something, any Leo will do. It's not my fault your parents actually called you Leo Secombe with no middle name."

Clearly there was no winning, so my only chance was to join her. I downed the rest of my wine and grimaced. "Do you want four-cheese pizza?"

"I want you to text him. Then we order pizza." I groaned, knowing damn well she wasn't going to let this go. She filled up my wine glass. "Text him. Short and sweet. Had a great time last night, thanks again." She nodded to my phone. "Quick. Now, before you have time to freak out about it."

Maybe she was right. Maybe the wine had gone to my head because I hadn't eaten all day. "Okay, okay." I opened my messages and clicked on his name and thumbed out a quick text.

Had a great time last night, and thanks again for driving me to work.

I hit Send before reason could catch up with my lack of common sense. "What if he doesn't reply?"

Kell looked at me very seriously and held up her glass. "Then we riot at dawn."

Nodding, I ordered the pizza and fell onto the couch.

I'd just kicked off my shoes when my phone beeped with a text.

Can I call you?

"Oh dear," I mumbled. "That's not ominous at all. He hates me. I should have known this would happen."

I held up my phone so Kell could see. "Type *yes*," she said. "See what he has to say before you torture yourself, and me by proxy."

I replied quickly, my stomach in knots. Maybe drinking wine without eating wasn't a good idea. *Sure.*

My phone rang almost immediately.

"Hey," he said softly. He sounded happy, which was a good sign. Confusing, but a good sign.

"Hey."

"I'm glad you texted me," he continued. Now I could barely hear him.

"Why are you whispering?"

"I'm still at dinner with my fam. I got your text and told them I needed to make a call and ducked outside. They're probably trying to listen through the wall."

I laughed, still a little confused. "Listen, I just wanted to apologise for last night," I said, just putting it right out there.

"What for?" He sounded genuinely surprised.

"Well, for being desperate and begging. Jesus. I respect your consent, and I'm sorry for pushing." I could feel my whole face burn, and Kell laughed. I gave her the bird. "I'm kinda embarrassed, to be honest."

"Don't be. Don't be embarrassed. I liked it. It bolstered my ego for like a decade, so I should probably thank you."

I snorted but now was even more confused. "So you didn't want to call me to tell me you don't want to see me again?"

"What?" he scoffed. "No. Hell no. Why would you

think that? I thought we hit it off great. Do you not think we got on well?"

"Yes! I do, absolutely. You're great, and I've been stressing all day that you probably thought I was some sex-crazed hooker."

He burst out laughing. "I don't think that at all. Though three times on one date might have set a precedent that I'm not sure I can live up to or maintain. Just so you know."

Now it was me who laughed. "Duly noted. And same, to be honest."

He was quiet for a moment, and I could almost see him smile. "The reason why I wanted to call you was to ask when I could see you again. If you want to, that is."

"Oh, I want to. And I'm not above begging, as we've clearly established."

He chuckled. "I really didn't think of it as begging, just so you know. I thought you might think I was a prude for setting boundaries."

"What? Oh my God, no. I would never think that." I sighed happily. "Boundaries are a good thing. I have some boundaries of my own, actually. But maybe we should talk about those face to face. Kell is sitting on the couch with me, listening intently to every word I say."

"I know your boundaries," Kell said, then speaking loud enough for Merrick to hear. "No olives on pizza. No chai lattes. No coriander on anything."

"I wasn't talking about those boundaries," I said with a laugh.

"Right," Merrick said. "I'm making a note. No olives, chai, or coriander. Tell Kell I said thanks. Though I'm curious about the other boundaries," he added. "When can I see you again. You're off on Tuesday, right? I could be free Tuesday afternoon as well?"

"Tuesday sounds great. Tell me when and where, and I'll be there."

AT THREE O'CLOCK, I pulled up at Merrick's ceramics studio. The plan was for me to meet him there and we'd go . . . Well, he didn't tell me where we were going. But the mystery kind of made it exciting.

Merrick had said his last class finished at three, so I wasn't surprised to find a whole bunch of people in the studio. But they appeared to be almost finished, tidying up and putting things away. They seemed a more experienced class, because they were using the pottery wheels, and I could see some pretty amazing bowls and vases being carefully taken into the drying room.

I ordered myself a coffee and had intended to sit at one of the tables in the café to wait until Merrick was done, but the lady behind the counter recognised me. She took my fiver with a curious smile. "You're Leo, right?"

"I am, yes."

"We haven't been officially introduced. I'm Ciara. Merrick told me to expect you," she said as she began to make my coffee. "He won't be long."

"Yeah, that's no problem. I think they're packing up in there now."

Ciara finished frothing the milk and poured it into my cup, then gave me a big smile. "So, big date, huh?"

Okay, so he'd obviously told Ciara about me. "Uh, yes. I think so, although I can't be sure because I have no idea where he's taking me. Should I be worried?" Oh God. "Am I dressed appropriately?" I was wearing dark blue denim jogger pants and a blue shirt with dozens of tiny cacti all over it.

She laughed and handed me my coffee. "You're dressed just fine."

"So you know where we're going? Can I get a clue?"

"Merrick would kill me if I told you. Not that I think he intended it to be a secret, but he was stressing about where to take you."

"Stressing? What for?"

She looked at me like I missed the obvious. "He was stressing about where to take you because what if you thought it was stupid, stressing about what to wear because everything he owns has clay on it, stressing about dinner."

Oh. "I didn't realise."

She glanced over my shoulder and whispered, "He wants to impress you." She looked right past me and smiled, and I realised a little belatedly that someone was coming up behind me.

I turned around and found Merrick walking over. Christ. How is it possible that he was even better looking today? Since when did clay-covered aprons become sexy? "Oh, hey," I said.

"Hey," he said, his eyes locked on mine. "I won't be long. I just need to finish up." He waved a hand back toward the studio. "Five minutes, okay?"

"Perfect."

He took a few backward steps toward the door to the studio and gave Ciara a look I couldn't quite decipher before he turned that killer smile back to me. "Don't believe a word she says."

He disappeared through the door and Ciara laughed. "Well, you don't have to believe me, but I can honestly say I haven't seen him smile like that at anyone in all the years I've known him."

I put my coffee back on the counter and sagged with a sigh. "I swear he gets fucking hotter every time I see him."

She burst out laughing and Merrick poked his head back around the doorway. He looked at us both for a long moment each. "Everything okay?"

She waved him off. "We're talking about you, not to you. You just hurry up in there."

He glowered at her but disappeared again just as some people from the pottery class came out. Ciara got busy with their coffee orders, so I took my coffee and sat at the table by the door to wait. Some more people left, some more people stayed for coffee and cake. They were varying in ages, from twenties to sixties, if I had to guess. But they each called out goodbye to Merrick and Ciara as they left, and everyone left smiling.

Eventually the lights in the studio went off and Merrick appeared, minus the apron, but he was wearing that gorgeous smile. "Sorry to keep you," he said with a gentle hand on my shoulder.

That touch, his dark eyes, his pink lips . . . It was all I could do to not melt on the spot. "It was no problem. Ciara makes really good coffee."

"Did she tell you horrible lies about me?"

"Not at all. Though she wouldn't tell me where we're going or what you have planned for us. Not even a clue."

He made a face. "If you hate it or if you think it's stupid, we can leave."

Oh God . . . "Okay, now you actually have me worried. You're not taking me to some live snake show, are you?"

"Uh no."

"And you're not going to make me watch live feeds of Parliament in session, are you?"

He chuckled. "Nope."

"Football?"

"Definitely not."

"Then it will be fine."

I finished my coffee and we waved goodbye to Ciara and slipped out the door. He stopped after he unlocked his car. "Maybe I should tell you now, in case you want to veto me, and we can go do something else."

God, he really was stressing about this. It was hard for me to imagine him stressing about anything. He always seemed so confident, and what did Ciara say? That he wanted to impress me? That did crazy things to the butter-flies in my belly. "I'm sure it'll be fine, Merrick."

"I booked us in at the go-kart track," he said, his face a mask of doubt and fear.

"Go-karts?"

He nodded. "Is it stupid? I tried to think of something that would be fun and different. I'm sorry. If you want to go down to the wharf—"

"It all depends, Merrick," I said, trying to play it cool.

"Depends on what?"

"On whether you're ready to get your arse kicked on the go-kart track." I laughed. "Go-karts sound awesome! I can't believe you were worried. I love it."

He sighed with relief, his grin wide. "Oh, thank God." He opened his car door and got in, so I did the same. "Hey," he whispered, leaning over the console as though he wanted to kiss me. I leaned in too and he put a hand to my cheek as our lips met. "I wanted to do that since I saw you talking to Ciara."

"I wouldn't have minded."

He smiled and his cheeks tinted. "Good to know." He started the car, but before we were even out on the street, he gave me that dazzling, shit-eating grin. "And just so you know, I'm going to beat you at go-karts. You don't stand a chance."

I laughed. "Well, I guess we're about to find out."

———

AS IT TURNED OUT, I was much better at go-karting than Merrick. He adamantly declared his go-kart was defective and the accelerator was slack, but I out-manoeuvred him around corners and beat him to the inside lane several times.

"You totally tried to take me out," Merrick said with a smile as we handed our helmets back.

"It was a fair corner."

He chuckled and gave my shoulder a gentle nudge. "Okay, I'll let you have this one. But at least I know for next time that fair and honourable tactics go out the window."

I snorted out a laugh. "You'll let me have this one? You'll *let* me? You know who else will let me? The scoreboard." I gestured broadly to the scoreboard above our heads. "Forever immortalised as the winner. See? It says right there. First place: Leo."

He laughed again. "Glad you're not one to gloat."

"I know, could you imagine?" We headed to the exit and I held the door for him. "This was a lot of fun, thank you. It was a great idea."

"It was fun, though next time I'll have to think of something I can actually win."

"Self-control. You won that one, hands down."

"It was tenuous at best." He unlocked the car and we got in. "I almost gave in. Just so you know."

I gasped. "Do you mean to say I only had to pout and beg one more time?"

"Not even beg. The pouting alone would've done it."

His cheeky smile told me he was joking, so I sighed dramatically. "Well, at least I know for next time that fair and honourable tactics go out the window."

He burst out laughing again and leaned over the console. "Kiss me."

I considered declining, and I considered giving him an almost kiss and then citing self-control, but in keeping with my playing dirty theme of the day, I pulled his face to mine and gave him the deepest, filthiest kiss I could manage. All tongue and obscene groans. His momentary shock melted away and he let me have my way with his mouth. When I pulled back, his eyes were closed, his mouth open, lips wet.

"How was that?" I asked.

His gaze was unfocused and a dopey smile spread across his face before he seemed to snap out of whatever trance he was in. "You really don't play fair," he said, squirming in his seat and then readjusting his crotch.

I chuckled victoriously. "Probably not. But I do like to win."

He started the car and shook his head, still smiling. "Promise me one thing."

"Sure."

"Promise me that after dinner tonight, you'll kiss me like that again."

I grinned. "Sure."

DINNER WAS two salads at a Greek restaurant and the food was divine, though Merrick was seemingly nervous about something. "You okay?" I asked.

"Yeah, sure," he replied, sipping his mineral water.

"You seem nervous."

"Well, I'm curious about something you said."

"What did I say?"

"You mentioned boundaries. Actually, there was a mention of foods you dislike and you said they weren't the boundaries you were talking about, which inferred there were other boundaries. And I was curious as to what they might be."

"Oh, *those* boundaries."

He took a mouthful of his dinner and chewed, never breaking eye contact with me. He waited for my answer.

Aw hell. Was it too early for this conversation? Was it too soon for us to be discussing this? From the way he was looking at me across the table, I would think not.

"I was referring to relationship boundaries."

He sipped his drink, ever so casually. "And what may they be?"

"Well, just general things. Expectations and things that I won't put up with. In relationships and prospective boyfriends, that kind of thing."

"Prospective boyfriends?"

"Hmm," I said, ignoring the way my face heated and how my belly swooped. "You know, if someone should be interested, that is."

He tried not to smile. "And if someone were perhaps interested? They should know what these boundaries are, correct?"

I tried not to smile right back at him. "It would be only fair."

"Okay Leo, you're killing me."

I sighed. "It's nothing major or scary. I don't think. I'm very tame by a lot of standards," I began. *Here goes nothing* . . . "I expect monogamy. Trust and loyalty are very important to me, and if I can't trust someone, it's over. I am who I am, and I won't change that for anyone. If my job or my friends aren't good enough, we're done. And I don't play second fiddle to anyone. I'm not an afterthought or a plan B. I mean, I don't expect anyone to move mountains for me, but I just won't be taken for granted or used until something better comes along. And I realise this makes me sound conceited and you probably think I'm asking for too much." I shrugged. "But while I expect these things for me, I give them back in return. I mean, relationships go both ways, right?"

Merrick didn't say anything for a long moment, and I had a godawful sinking feeling that he didn't agree . . . But then he reached across the table and took my hand. "You're not asking for too much, Leo. You just want respect, for yourself and what's important to you. And I'm sorry if some dickbag hurt you and ever made you think your self-respect was optional."

His words hit me like a sledgehammer. My heart squeezed and my eyes burned, and I had to will my tears away.

CHAPTER FOURTEEN

MERRICK

LEO'S *BOUNDARIE*S told me that someone had hurt
him. It all basically boiled down to him wanting a boyfriend
who didn't cheat on him or make him feel like shit. It was
pretty sad that he had to set rules for things that should have
been, for me at least, common decency.

"I've been on dates with guys who seemed to think that
being a bottom equals being a doormat," he said sadly.

I shook my head. "They weren't worth your time, Leo.
You're so much better than that. You deserve better than
that."

He eventually smiled and squeezed my hand. "Thank
you."

"So can I share my boundaries with you?" I asked. "You
know, in case there's a prospective boyfriend within
earshot."

He looked at the closest table near us, where a man who
had to be in his eighties, at least, was seated. "Sure. Though
you might need to speak up so he can hear you. He's pretty
old."

I laughed, but he hooked his foot around mine under the table and gave me his undivided attention.

"Well," I started. "I agree with the monogamy thing. It's about trust and respect, and that's important to me as well. And . . ." Here was the big one. "I would need any prospective boyfriend to understand that my business is very important to me. It doesn't mean you would be second fiddle, Leo, because you wouldn't be. It's just that I have business commitments and responsibilities that can sometimes take up a lot of my time, and it's not that one would be more important than the other, it's just about finding balance."

Leo smiled. "I get that. And your business *is* important, and you've worked hard to get it where it is. I would never ask you to choose. But like you said, balance is good."

"My brother keeps telling me that I'm allowed to have both a business and a boyfriend."

He smiled, his eyes warm. "Your brother sounds like a smart guy."

"He's smart, yes. But he's kinda bossy and nosy too. He wants to meet you."

Leo's eyes went wide. "He does?"

"Sure." I laughed. "Oh, and another boundary, though this reads more like a prospective-boyfriend, fine-print terms and conditions clause . . . My family. They're all kind of overbearing, nosy, loud, and opinionated. So any potential boyfriend would, and duly should, be aware of what he's getting himself into. There will be an interrogation at some point, a few rounds of twenty-questions, that kind of thing."

He looked slightly horrified. "On a scale of one to Targaryen, just how scary are we talking?"

I laughed. "Targaryen? God, you'll fit right in."

He sighed loudly, but a smile tugged at his lips. "I don't mind. You'll—I mean, any prospective boyfriend—would have to meet Kell too. Oh, and my family, but they're easy. As long as I'm happy, they are too."

"Is Kell scary?"

"Hungover, yes. And when she's hungry, yes. Otherwise she's fine."

"Right," I said. "So, bring cake."

Leo laughed. "Oh, you are good."

Our gazes met and I couldn't make myself look away. His blue eyes were like a tropical ocean: warm and inviting. I wanted to wade into the depths and drown in him. I swallowed hard. "You ready to go?"

He nodded quickly. "I believe I have a kissing agreement to fulfil." His voice was thick, and full of promise. "And I've never broken a promise."

We halved the bill and hightailed it out of there. I was already getting turned on just imagining what we were going to do. "My place?" I asked as I started the car.

He nodded quickly. "My car's at your place, so if you wanted to go to my place, we'd have to swing past your place first, which would be totally fine if you wanted to do that, but it just seems like a waste of time when that time could be spent much more productively doing other things."

I chuckled, agreeing wholeheartedly. "Time management is very important."

There was no nervousness this time when we got to the front door of the studio. I let Leo in first, fixed the security code, and locked the door behind us before leading him up the stairs. The lamp was on, casting a glow of orange light against the darkness. Long shadows moved across the walls, and my heartbeat echoed loud in the silence. Could he hear that? How could he not?

"Can I get you a drink?" I asked.

"No, thanks," he whispered. "Not a drink."

"Then what?"

"Your mouth," he murmured as he cupped my face and kissed me. I had asked him to kiss me the way he had in the car, and that's what he did. Demanding and deep, controlling and caressing at the same time. His tongue danced with mine, tasting and teasing, and when I thought he might stop for air, he kissed me deeper and harder. Still holding my face, he was in total control, moving my jaw as he wanted, getting the angle he needed to give me his tongue. It was an onslaught of sensation. My knees were weak, my dick was hard, and my balls ached. My heart raced and my head swam.

I wanted him to kiss me like this forever, but I needed air. I broke the kiss and gasped in a breath, and he grinned, smug and victorious.

"Fuck, you're hot," he mumbled before kissing me again.

My God, his mouth . . . his tongue and his hands . . . He was going to bring me to orgasm without even touching my cock.

I pulled back with more force this time and gripped his chin between my thumb and forefinger. "Your mouth," I breathed. "Your tongue. Those lips."

He grinned, dark-eyed and swollen lipped. "Want some more?"

I stared at him, burning with desire and lust, with the need to come. "Get on your knees."

His nostrils flared and his breath hitched, but he slowly dropped to his knees. Right there, beside my couch. I unzipped my jeans and he gasped, and I freed my aching cock. I thumbed his bottom lip and he opened his mouth and took me in. Wet heat engulfed me, and I cried out with the pleasure of it.

I wouldn't be lasting long tonight.

And like he knew his prize was close, Leo sucked hard and took me all the way in. He gripped my arse and pulled me into his throat, and I came so hard and fast, the room spun. Lights danced behind my eyes as my orgasm detonated throughout every cell of my body. He drank every drop.

My fucking God.

I rocked back on my heels, unsteady, and Leo grabbed me, getting to his feet with a very smug smile. "You okay there?"

"No. I have wobbly bones and I don't even know how I'm standing."

Leo laughed as he pulled me into his embrace. God, he felt so good against me, his arms wrapped around me just right. His lips found mine, and the ferocity of his kiss surprised me . . . until the hard press of his cock against my hip registered in my orgasm-hazy brain.

I slid my hand between us, palming him, and his kiss stuttered.

"Sit on the couch," I ordered.

"You're bossy tonight," he murmured, his voice thick and his eyes dark with desire.

"I'm bossy every night," I replied, urging to him to sit with my hand on his shoulder.

His smile became wicked. "Don't tease me."

I chuckled as I went to my knees between his legs. I pulled his jogger pants down, just far enough to reveal his briefs. The elastic of his pants stretched across his thighs and restricted how far he could spread his legs. He groaned with frustration, so I pulled his arse forward on the couch, and then he groaned with pleasure.

He liked being manhandled, and he liked having a

bossy top. Not that I didn't doubt he wouldn't be a bossy-as-hell bottom, but I really liked how he responded to me. I nuzzled his erection through his briefs and he pulled his shirt up and flexed his hips forward. He whined with frustration and a dot of precome darkened his briefs.

Oh yeah.

I dragged his briefs down at the front, leaving him confined around the thighs, and took his painfully hard erection into my mouth. He was salty and sweet and trying to writhe and thrust. I held his hips in place and worked him long and hard, sucking his orgasm out of him. He cried out as he came, convulsing with the force of it.

When I released him, he sagged, seemingly unable to speak. I climbed up on the couch and pulled him into a lying position, kissing him lazily until he came back to earth. I put my hand to his face and through his hair, gentle traces and nose nudges, which led to more smiling kisses.

It was ridiculous how perfectly we fit together. How comfortable it was.

How right it felt.

"I thought we were supposed to be talking," Leo murmured dreamily. His eyelids opened slowly, and he smiled. "Not that I'm opposed to all the orgasms."

I chuckled. "I want to talk but keep getting distracted by how much you turn me on."

"Sorry about that."

"No you're not."

"No, I'm really not." He kissed me. "What did you want to talk about?"

"Anything, everything, and nothing in particular." I traced my finger along his eyebrow. "Your job, your friends, your family, your favourite book or TV show. The TV show you hated that everyone else loved. The most played song on your playlist. That kind of stuff."

He snuggled in closer, our hips flush, and he rubbed my back. He pulled down a cushion and shoved it under his head, and when he was comfy, he began to talk.

We talked about anything, everything, and nothing in particular for hours. We discussed who and what he liked about his job and who and what he didn't. He told me about his friends who he doesn't see nearly enough and how he got into the Bridge-the-Gap program. We discussed the political and social structure of *Star Wars* and how his favourite playlist on Spotify was a mix of Creedence Clearwater Revival, the Beach Boys, Cher, and Post Malone.

Then we laughed about which movies had scared us when we were kids and which celebrities we secretly crushed on and when we'd first realised we were gay.

And it was there, on my couch at almost one in the morning, with the faint glow of light outlining his face when he was laughing about some hot surfer guy on *Home and Away* that he used to drool over when he was thirteen, that I knew I was falling in love with Leo Secombe.

Was it fast and reckless and completely irrational?

Maybe.

Did that change anything?

No.

". . . and there was this one scene where he came walking out of the ocean with his surfboard, dripping wet and wearing nothing but boardies, that I had my come-to-gay-Jesus realisation because—"

I cupped his face and kissed him, unable to help myself. *My God, I was falling in love with him.* I rolled on top of him, kissing him harder and deeper, and his surprise melted away and he kissed me back. He spread his legs as much as the couch allowed, and I slotted against him so perfectly. He slid a hand up under my shirt and moaned into my mouth.

It wasn't just desire that curled in my belly. I had butterflies too, and my heart was thumping hard against my ribs. The jittery excitement of new love, of possibility. It was absolutely terrifying and exhilarating. And scary and wonderful.

He slowed the kiss before we could get too carried away. "Was it something I said?"

"It was everything you said."

Leo smiled beautifully. His eyes darted between mine, searching, and I wondered if he could see this new realisation in the way I looked at him.

"I have to be at work at eight thirty," he whispered. "I should probably get going."

"Or you could stay here," I suggested. "I can lend you a shirt."

He bit his bottom lip and his eyes glittered with humour. "I should go. Because if we get in your bed, I'll be begging you again to fuck me."

My hips rolled and my cock jerked at his words, which he very clearly felt. "And maybe this time I won't be saying no."

He whispered, "It's late already . . ."

"And when it does happen," I said, kissing him softly and thumbing his cheek, "I want to take my time. I want it to last for hours so your body never forgets mine."

He closed his eyes slowly, his nostrils flared, and he made a pained sound in the back of his throat. "Holy shit. Yeah, okay. You keep talking like that, and I won't be going anywhere."

I pulled back and dragged myself off him, which my

body did not want to do. I moved to the end of the couch. "Sorry."

He sat up and readjusted his crotch. "No, don't be sorry. Being in a permanent state of turned-on isn't completely torturous. I mean, there are worse ways to die, right?"

I chuckled. "Are you sure you're okay to go home?"

He nodded. "Yep."

"I'll walk you out."

I led the way downstairs to the front door. I took care of the security code and leaned against the door. "When will I see you again?"

"Friday," he replied. "Clyde and I have some very important glazing and pottery work to do."

"Sounds like fun."

"It is. The teacher is a total hottie." He stepped in real close, pressing me against the door. "I'm going to need you to step aside so I can leave. Unless you *really* want me to stay . . . ?"

I groaned and moved to the side, opening the door. "I'm questioning all my life choices right now."

He laughed and pressed his lips to mine. "Goodnight, Merrick."

"Night, Leo."

———

FRIDAY COULDN'T COME QUICK ENOUGH. Leo and I had texted several times, and we'd spoken on the phone once, and that was great and all . . . but I really just wanted to see him.

"You keep looking at the door," Uncle Donny said. He had arrived later than normal and had noticeably avoided any eye contact and ignored my probing for details on his phone number exchange with Clyde.

"I assume we're waiting on the same two people to arrive," I replied quietly. "Even though you won't give me any details."

"A gentleman never kisses and tells."

I almost dropped the freshly glazed pot I was holding. "You've kissed him?" I whisper-hissed. No one else could hear us; they were all chatting at the long table and we were near the sinks. "Uncle Donny, you need to spill the details."

He smiled like he knew a sordid secret that I didn't. Which was exactly what this was. "A gentleman never tells." He sipped his coffee. "And anyway, you haven't spilled any details about how things are progressing with your new man."

"He is . . . Well, he is . . ."

"He is here," Uncle Donny said quietly, and sure enough, when I looked up, Leo and Clyde had arrived. "And I can tell by your smile how things are with him."

Uncle Donny turned and walked toward them, silently taking his seat next to Clyde. "Morning," Clyde said.

Uncle Donny replied with just a nod, but there was an unfamiliar set to his lips that resembled a shy smile. Anyone else might have missed it, but I certainly did not.

"Not the last one in today," Shirley said.

"Couldn't wait to see you, Shirl," Clyde replied. "I missed your article in *Bitter People* this week. Was wondering if you were okay."

She smiled, even laughed a little. "Oh, sorry. This week's write-up went to *How to Deal with Idiots*. Shame you missed it, because you got a mention."

Clyde grinned at her and everyone just smiled, because this was how they were.

"Morning," Leo said, ignoring Clyde and Shirley's exchange.

His smile made my heart thump around in my chest. I wanted to reach out and touch him and kiss him but settled on a polite greeting instead. "Hey."

"Oh," Shirley said musically. "Maybe I should write an article for *Young Love*, called 'When Boys Look at Each Other Like That.'"

Leo and I both turned to the table and, sure enough, every pair of eyes were on us. I laughed, my cheeks going red, and I was suddenly out of breath. God, had I inhaled at all since he walked in? I couldn't remember.

Leo cleared his throat and took his seat. He was embarrassed too and trying not to smile. "Good morning, Shirley. You look lovely today."

"Leo, I keep telling you not to lie," Clyde chimed in.

Shirley smiled and eloquently raised her middle finger at Clyde just as the last two people arrived, quickly taking their seats, and it was time for the class to begin. "What did we miss?" Joan asked, looking between Shirley and Clyde.

The entire table answered with a resounding, "Nothing."

I chuckled at their antics. Sure, there was some antagonising and jibing, but the group were very clearly friends. I enjoyed this class immensely, and not just for having Leo in it. "Morning everyone," I said. "Today we're finishing off our bowls, which we made last week. But first we get to see how our pinch pots turned out from the kiln."

I carried the large covered tray over to the work table and slid it into the middle. I began to lift the plastic cover up, then stopped. "Okay, before we see these, just remember that we have no way to know exactly how the firing process will affect the clay or the glaze. There's just no guarantee. Even after all these years, when I do my own, I can't say for certain how they'll look exactly."

"Is this your way of saying some of our pots are awful?" Harvey asked.

"No," I replied. "Well. Not . . . awful. But at least we had no explosions." There were a few laughs and I lifted the cover to reveal all the cute little different coloured pots. "They actually turned out really great."

Everyone took theirs, happily examining their handiwork. Some were better than others, admittedly, I couldn't help but notice. Clyde's was a standout; he had a natural talent for ceramics.

Leo's was at the other end of the scale. It was kinda lumpy, uneven, and the layered blue glazing only seemed to highlight its . . . originality. But he held it and smiled at it like it was the most precious thing. "Look!" he said to Clyde. Then he showed me. "Look! Isn't he cute?"

Right then and there, my heart had pretty much decided for me. It did some stuttering hammer-squeezy dance in my chest, and I laughed. "He's just the cutest."

I wasn't talking about his pot. He knew it, I knew it, and apparently everyone else in the class knew it, but I couldn't bring myself to care. He *was* the cutest.

"Ah, Merrick. Should we start on the bowls?" Joan asked.

Apparently I was just staring at Leo and his little blue pot, smiling like the village idiot. "In the drying room," I answered, distracted and trying to catch up.

A warm hand clapped my shoulder. It was Harvey. "Son, you got it bad. Leo, give this man your phone number so he can function."

"They don't do phone numbers anymore," Clyde declared. "They do this thing called 'swiping right.'"

Leo blushed, and I'm sure it matched mine, and all the younger people smiled, but everyone collected their bowls and continued to work on them as talk at the table soon turned to dating forty years ago compared to today. It was engaging and funny, and everyone joined in as though they'd known each other forever. Uncle Donny never spoke at all but he smiled a lot, and it was more than I'd seen him smile in . . . well, ever.

And every so often Leo would catch my eye and smile. My fucking heart was going to stampede right out of my chest, and my stupid belly kept flipping and swooping every single time.

I shook my head and took a deep breath, drawing my focus back to the class. Some added patterns to their bowls with modelling tools, some pressed patterns in with stamps, and some were going to paint patterns with glaze. Leo opted not to pattern his and wanted to use different coloured glazes, whereas Clyde matched his to the little perfect pot he'd made.

We got the pots all into the drying room and there was still just over half an hour to go of their class. "I want to show you guys something," I said, holding a lump of clay I'd been wedging as we talked. "Come this way." I walked to my potter's wheel and sat down. "I want to show you how to throw. Then next week you can all have a go at doing it yourselves."

"Throw?" Shirley asked.

"Yep. We call it throwing clay or throwing pots. Something to do with the old English word that means to turn." I got myself comfortable and centred at the wheel. I threw the clay onto the wheel-head. It was second nature to me, like breathing, and sometimes I forgot that it was new to other people.

133

I pounded the clay, thumping it a few times with the heel of my hand. "We just need to make sure it's secure," I explained, then dipped my hands in the tub of slip. "This is slip. A mix of water and clay that acts as the lubricant."

Leo snorted. "Don't try that at home, boys and girls."

I laughed and started the wheel on a medium speed. "I need to brace my elbows on my knees like this and hold the clay between both hands. Then I want to gently squeeze." The clay began to take shape. "And using both hands, I want to pull it up."

"That's what he said," Harvey said.

It always did look a little phallic at this point. I laughed, then with some more slip, pushed the clay back down slowly. "This is called centring. Keeping equal pressure and weight distribution, we want to bring it back down to the wheel." I added a little more slip. "Now we want to begin forming the hole. Make sure it's nice and wet."

"We're all familiar with that," Joan said.

"I had no idea this would be so sexual," Shirley added.

I looked up at my audience then, smiling, until my gaze fell on Leo. He was staring at my hands, his cheeks flushed, his lips open, his eyes dark.

I knew that look.

Christ.

I almost lost my centre but quickly focused back on my task, trying to keep my voice even. "Okay, now I want to press the heel of my left hand against the outside and, reaching in, let my two fingers begin to form and pull the hole."

Someone snorted.

"God, these jokes just write themselves," Clyde said.

I laughed again but didn't dare look up. "And then I want to slow the wheel down as I bring the edges up."

Everyone watched in silence until I drew my fingers up the sides and said, "I need to ease off the pressure as I get to the rim and go back to the base for another long and slow pull upwards."

Then everyone cracked up laughing and I had to stop and laugh too. Leo was laughing as well but his cheeks were still pink, and when his gaze met mine, there was definitely something there.

Did me throwing a pot turn him on?

He licked his lips, and his eyes went to my hands again and he inhaled.

Yep. He liked it.

Jesus.

It took me a second to regroup, and I finished the pot. I had to smooth the rim with my finger, but there was no way I was saying that. I wired it off the wheel and gently twist-lifted it. "Ta-da!"

I received a round of applause from my class; even Leo managed a distracted clap. The pot itself wasn't anything special, but there was something magical about turning a lump of clay into something usable, practical, recognisable.

"Next week you can all try your hand at throwing," I explained.

"And it will be just as easy as you made it look, won't it?" Shirley asked jokingly.

"I've been doing this for years," I admitted. "I might have made it look a little easy. But it's a lot of fun."

Everyone left very happy and excited, except for Leo, Clyde, and Uncle Donny, who waited while I cleaned up and washed my hands. Leo joined me at the sink. "So that was . . . Um."

"Interesting?"

"I was going to say great, but yeah, interesting." He

chewed on his bottom lip and shook his head. "I had no idea it was so . . ."

I dried my hands on a towel, casting a casual glance at Clyde and Uncle Donny to see them talking quietly and not listening to us. "I could tell you liked it."

"It was very sensual," he whispered. "I wasn't expecting it to be . . . like that."

"Sensual? I've never thought of it that way."

"How can you not? Jesus, it was better than porn."

I laughed, earning us a glance from Clyde and Uncle Donny before they went back to their conversation. "Right, then. Duly noted," I said quietly.

"Though it makes sense now," he mused. "How muscly your arms and shoulders are. How incredibly talented you are with your hands."

I laughed, despite the burn in my belly and chest. "I do like to be thorough."

He laughed out a quiet groan. "Can I see you later?"

"God, yes. I have another class but should be free by five-ish."

"Perfect." He swallowed hard. "Dinner, and my place would probably be a better option. Because I'm pretty sure if we come back here, I'll insist we play 'Unchained Melody' while we re-enact the pottery scene from *Ghost*, but we'll be naked and there will be all-over clay body masks, which will lead to mud wrestling where your dick could accidently slide into my arse a lot, for hours and hours, and you'll never look at your lovely wooden work table the same ever again," he said with a grin. "Nor would you be able to explain the splatter of clay and my arseprints over every flat surface."

I chuckled again. "Is that right?"

"Yep. It'd be a mess, but wow, we'd have great skin."

God, he made me laugh. "So, dinner at your place?"

He nodded. "Kell will probably be there, so it's great you might get to meet her, but that eliminates any chance of hand jobs on the couch."

I barked out a laugh and reached for him, just putting my hand on his arm.

"Merrick," Uncle Donny said, interrupting us. I dropped my hand. Both he and Clyde were now standing. "I'm leaving. Thank you again for your class today."

"Oh, sure," I said, wanting desperately to speak more with him, but Uncle Donny simply gave me and Leo a nod before he turned and walked out.

"Everything okay, Clyde?" Leo asked.

"Yep. Why wouldn't it be?" he groused. "You ready to go, Leo? We got groceries to get yet."

Leo gave me an uncertain look. "That doesn't sound good. I'll text you," he whispered before following Clyde to the exit. "Oh, and thank you for the class today. It was very . . . educational."

He grinned before disappearing out through the café. I sighed happily and began cleaning up, getting ready for my next class.

CHAPTER FIFTEEN

LEO

"WHAT HAPPENED WITH DONNY?" I asked, after a few moments of brooding silence from Clyde.

"Nothing, why?"

"You both seemed a little . . ." I searched for the right word . . . disgruntled, terse, tense . . . "Unhappy."

"Just a bit of nunya, that's all."

"Nunya?"

"Yeah. Nunya fucking business," he replied. I laughed, because that was typical Clyde, and the corner of his mouth curled upward. "We're just fine. Nothing for you to worry about. What's going on between you and Merrick is a better question. Thought you were gonna mess yourself when he was making that pot."

"Was that not the hottest thing you've ever seen?"

Clyde turned slowly to look at me like I'd sprouted a second head. "Not even close, Leo. Not even close."

I chuckled. "Pretty sure I'll be asking for private lessons, if you know what I mean. Do you think if I bathe myself in clay he'd finally work me over like he did that pot?"

He furrowed his brow. "What do you mean 'finally'?"

Oh shit.

"Nothing, no I just meant—"

"You mean to tell me you two haven't got that far yet?" His bushy eyebrows almost met. "You've been on what? Three or four dates? Jecz, back in my day we didn't waste time like that."

I shifted in my seat. "Well, it's not for the lack of my trying or wanting it. And he does too. We've done . . . stuff. Basically everything except *actual* sex. But we're trying to establish an actual relationship, not just sex." I cleared my throat. "You know, a lot of guys don't ever have anal sex, Clyde. It's not the pinnacle of expression." I was very well aware of how my argument with Clyde made me a hypocrite, but Merrick was right and I'd been wrong. Hearing myself say it now confirmed that.

He harrumphed and turned back to look out the windscreen. "I know that. But you want him to?"

"Well, I wouldn't say no."

"So what you want in this relationship isn't as important as what he wants?"

I sighed. "It's not like that."

"How is it not?"

"Because asking him to do something with his body that he's not comfortable in doing just yet is a little more significant than, say, telling me about his childhood fears. We're not sharing tacos, Clyde. It's about respecting boundaries and honesty. And consent. He was honest with me in telling me that he wanted to wait, and I respect that."

Clyde sighed. "Well, if you're sure. As long as he respects your wishes too. I just don't want to see you get hurt. I can tell how much you like him."

I pulled the car into a spot at the supermarket and

scrubbed a hand over my face. This conversation was so weird. "Want to tell me what's really bothering you?"

"Nope."

"Are you and Donny . . . dating? And don't you dare tell me it's a case of nunya."

He gave me a smile. "I wouldn't call it . . . dating. But we are mutually respectful of each other's needs and wants."

I sighed, long and loud. "Anyone ever told you you're insufferable?"

"Only on the days where I interact with other people."

I snorted and shook my head. "Can't imagine why." I pulled the keys out of the ignition. "Come on. Grocery time. I have a date to get ready for."

Clyde smiled as we walked into the supermarket, and he even smiled as we made our way down each aisle. He didn't even grumble about the bread, and he bought a name brand of loose-leaf tea, so something was *definitely* weird. He also needed to grab some toiletries, and I waited, without comment, while he chose a new toothbrush, new hand soap, and new razors. But then he stopped and sniffed some body wash, and things were most definitely weird. "You okay?" I asked.

"Are there laws against using this?" He held up the pink floral-scented body wash.

"No, not at all." I pulled down a mesh body puff. "But you might want to throw in one of these. You need to pour a dollop of the body wash onto the puff thing, then you wash your body with that."

He gave a nod. "Yeah, of course. I knew that." He very clearly did not know that. He returned to looking at all the products, and I realised then that he was buying these things to impress Donny. New personal hygiene routines were a dead giveaway. I should have realised sooner.

Then he stopped at the lube and condom section. Oh, Christ. *Was he . . . ? Did he . . . ?* I tried not to think about that because the accompanying visual was like imagining my grandpa . . . yeah, no thanks. I tried to act cool about it. "Silicone-based ones are better for—" I stopped talking when he gave me a raised eyebrow.

"I was buying this stuff before you were born, son," he replied, throwing a bottle in the trolley.

I gave him a deadpan glare and threw some in for myself, plus a pack of condoms. "What?" I asked. "Just because we're waiting for now doesn't mean we'll wait forever."

Clyde grinned. "Optimism in the face of adversity."

"Shut up."

He laughed. "Okay, now I need birdseed. Do they sell birdseed here?"

Okay, things were now past weird. "What do you want birdseed for?"

"Have you seen the price of chicken? I was going to plant it and grow my own." He shook his head. "Christ almighty, Leo. What do you think I want birdseed for?"

I shook my head. "God only knows," I whispered to him. "But if you plan on going to the park to feed the pigeons, just remember, you'll have better luck if you don't yell at them."

"I only yelled at the ones who tried to roost on my balcony."

"Mm-hmm." I sighed again, giving up any point of anything. I began pushing the trolley. "It's in the aisle with the dog food."

We collected the birdseed and got through the check

out without Clyde insulting anyone, which was like some kind of miracle. I helped him carry his groceries up to his apartment, and something seemed . . . different.

Had he cleaned? Used an air freshener? It was a nice change, whatever it was.

"Well," I said with my keys in my hand, walking to his front door. "If you want someone to go to the park with you, just let me know."

"The park?"

"To feed the birds."

"Oh." He huffed and almost smiled. "Sure. Whatever."

I opened the door but stopped before I stepped over the threshold. "You sure you're okay, Clyde?"

"Yeah, why wouldn't I be?"

"I dunno. You just . . . if you ever want to talk about anything, you can call me. Or if you want, I can make an appointment at Arcus and get you in there to see a counsellor. It's no problem."

"Quit your worryin', boy. Everything's fine."

"Okay." I tried for a smile. "I'll catch you soon."

He grumbled a goodbye and shooed me away, so I went home, a little confused and a lot concerned. But he was a grown man, and if he said he was fine, I would need to take his word for it. So I concentrated on my plans for the night. I texted Merrick my unit number and told him I was cooking dinner. He replied with 5:30 and a smiley face. It did stupid things to my insides.

If Merrick was coming here for dinner, I wanted to impress him, but I also wanted him to see the real me. I tidied up, cleaned and vacuumed, and this time I did change my sheets and remade my bed. Even if we didn't end up in bed tonight, he would at least see my room from the door when I gave him the very quick tour. I straightened up my bedside table, wiping the dust off it, when Clyde's words came back to me.

So what you want in this relationship isn't as important as what he wants?

What I had replied to Clyde was true. Relationships had to be based on boundaries and honesty, and I stood by that. But what he'd said had stung.

I didn't just want sex. I wanted everything with Merrick. I wanted the relationship he was trying to forge, and I wanted things to be long-term with him. I understood why he'd put up these boundaries.

But the rejection had stung, regardless of it being justified, even though we'd talked about it afterward and he'd apologised. He'd told me he *did* want me, and I knew he did. He never tried to hide his attraction to me: sexual, physical, emotional.

So why was I still stuck on this?

I wasn't sure, but maybe talking things out with Merrick tonight was a good idea.

Distracting myself, I set about peeling potatoes for the potato bake and remembered to give Kell a heads-up about tonight. Even though I knew she couldn't reply straight away, at least she'd know before she walked through the door. I shot her a quick text:

Jsyk, Merrick is coming over for dinner. I'm making chicken schnitty, taterbake and salad.

Her reply came through at 5:01. *OMG I love you. I'm starving!*

Then another text just a moment later. *Wait. Am I invited to this?*

I laughed and replied. *Of course. I want you to meet him.*

I could almost hear her reply. *Oooooh, getting serious!*

My smile kind of died, and my heart sank. Were we getting serious? I thought so. I wanted to be. I wanted everything with him, but there felt like something holding us back. *Well, we'll see.*

See you soon!

I put the potato bake in the oven and had a quick shower to freshen up. I changed into some jogger shorts and a button-down shirt with pineapples on it and had just finished brushing my teeth when the intercom door buzzer rang.

Shit!

I was certain it was him but pressed the intercom button. "Hello?"

"Uh, hi." Merrick's voice was silky smooth and I could tell he was smiling. "I was wondering if you could help me, I was looking for this really cute guy."

I laughed and let him in, then opened the door and waited for him. I heard the elevator ding and he came around the corner, and oh boy, his smile when he saw me . . .

That couldn't be faked, right?

That unbidden reaction was real. It had to be.

"Hey," he said. His voice felt like velvet.

"Hi."

He stepped right in close, close enough to kiss, but he waited. His freshly showered smell wafted over me and I hummed just as he pressed his lips to mine.

Fucking hell.

I wanted him already. I wanted him to touch, kiss, lick every part of me. I wanted him inside me so bad, I ached for it.

And we hadn't even got through the door yet.

"Christ, you're gonna kill me," I mumbled, taking a step back. "Come on in."

He stepped inside and the door closed behind him. "I brought you this," he said, holding up his closed fist. "I was going to get you flowers. I mean, you're cooking dinner so that would be the correct etiquette. Or so my mother says. And I like flowers, but I wanted to get you something more . . . me."

"More you?"

He nodded and opened his hand. A tiny clay figurine sat on his palm. Not just any kind of clay figurine, but a tiny lion. It was almost a terracotta colour, with a little mane and big round eyes. It was very round, shaped and carved from one piece, its features pinched and etched into place, and it looked just like a cross between a child's toy and a cartoon character. It was quite possibly the cutest thing I'd ever seen.

"I made it last week, but it wasn't ready until today."

My eyes shot to his. "You made this?"

He nodded slowly. "Well, yeah. It didn't take long and the class was working on their hand-building and I had a small lump of dried earthenware that was ready for finishing, and before I knew it, I'd made a little lion."

"For me?"

"Yeah. Because your name's Leo." He paused. "If you don't like it . . ."

"Are you kidding? It's gorgeous. I'm . . . stunned. Speechless. No one's ever . . ." I let out a rush of breath. "My God, Merrick. I love it."

His whole face lit up. "Oh, thank fuck for that. I thought for one horrifying moment that I should have gone with the flowers."

"Flowers are fine," I said, still looking at the little lion.

"Great, even, but they don't even compare." I met his gaze, my heart thumped, and my stomach was in knots. "Thank you."

"You're very welcome. I can make you the entire ark if you want."

I laughed at the thought. "Well, I wouldn't say no, but you don't need to do that. This little guy right here is just perfect." I held it on my palm between us. "I can't believe you made him for me."

"I love what I do, so it really was no bother. I'm just glad you like it."

I gently put the little lion on the kitchen bench and took Merrick's hand, pulling him close. I cupped his face with one hand. "Thank you," I murmured before kissing him. He pulled our bodies together and deepened the kiss just as we heard keys jangling at the door.

We broke apart as Kell came in. "Oh God, something smells so good." She stopped mid-stride, staring at us but mostly at Merrick. "Oh, hi. I'm Kell. Clearly I interrupted something because you both look like you got caught with your hands in the cookie jar. I mean, I totally get it. Leo *is* a snack."

Merrick laughed and offered his hand. "Merrick. Nice to meet you, Kell. And yes, he's a snack."

She shook his hand and grinned. "A snack who cooks dinner." She gave me an approving look. "It smells good, Leo. I'm just gonna go change. I need to get out of my trained monkey suit."

She disappeared down the hall and Merrick gave me a nervous smile. "I think that went okay?" he whispered.

I gave him a quick kiss. "You have nothing to worry about. Well, unless you count eating my cooking."

He smiled and seemed to relax a little. "It does smell good."

"That's just the potato bake. I hope you don't mind carbs and saturated fats. Though there's also a salad, so that makes it okay, right?"

"Perfect."

"Can I get you a drink?"

"Sure."

"Lemon mineral water, bottled water, Moscato, Diet Coke?"

"Ah, wine would be great."

I took out the bottle and grabbed three glasses. "Kell?" I yelled out. "Want a wine?"

She yelled back, "Does a one-legged duck swim in a circle?"

Merrick chuckled. "I believe that's a yes."

I laughed and poured three glasses. Kell came back out wearing sweatpants and a baggy T-shirt. "Sorry, Merrick," she said. "Friday night means no bra and elastic-waisted pants."

He laughed and handed her a wine. "Don't apologise. No bras and stretchy pants are compulsory Friday-night attire."

She clinked her glass to his. "I will drink to that."

I picked up my little lion. "Kell, look. Merrick brought this for me instead of flowers. He made it."

She gasped and took it, inspecting its details. Then she turned to Merrick. "You didn't."

He nodded. "I did."

I thought Kell was going to burst. "Oh my heart," she cried. "It's the cutest thing. A teeny tiny Leo the lion."

God, was she getting teary? She put the figurine down

gently. "Leo, you can stop trying. He wins. You'll never beat that."

"I'm not even going to try," I boasted.

Merrick was blushing. "I dunno, Leo. No one's ever made me dinner before, so . . ."

"Never?" Kell and I said in unison.

He shook his head. "Never."

I cringed. "Well, if I'd known that, I would have made something a little fancier."

"Are you kidding?" Merrick said. "Chicken schnitty, potato bake, and salad just might be the best dinner ever."

Kell raised her glass to me. "He's definitely a keeper."

I thought my heart just might stop beating. My earlier worries were long forgotten. Would we need to talk about expectations, personal and sexual? Sure. But that could wait for now. Because at the end of the day, even if Merrick never wanted to have anal sex, it wouldn't change anything for me and I knew that now. Was he definitely a keeper? My heart answered for me. *Yes. Yes, he was.*

THROUGHOUT DINNER, Kell subjected Merrick to a barrage of questions, most of which I knew the answer to, some I didn't. He played along good-naturedly, and I'd even guess that they liked each other. There were a lot of laughs, and when our plates were empty, we simply set them aside and kept on talking.

Eventually, though, when the dining chairs had outworn their comfort, we ended up on the couch. I took the long lounge and Merrick sat himself right next to me. Not creepy close, but close enough that when he rested his elbow on the back of the seat, his hand touched my shoulder.

Kell went into the kitchen. "Who wants another drink?"

Merrick gave me a questioning look. "I, uh, I probably shouldn't . . . if I'm driving home?"

"You're more than welcome to stay," I replied. "I mean, it would go against my civic duty to allow you to drink and drive."

He smiled, his gaze meeting mine, and neither one of us could look away. "I should go home tonight," he replied. "But thank you for your civic duty." I couldn't hide my disappointment but I didn't push.

"Just water, thanks," I called back to Kell.

He snatched up my hand. "Next time."

I nodded. "Next time."

He brought my hand to his lips and kissed my palm. "I don't want to rush this, Leo," he whispered. "I think we could really have something here."

"Me too," I replied, my heart in my throat. "Can we talk about something later?"

His gaze shot to mine, a little panicked. "Sure."

"It's nothing bad," I said, leaning over to kiss him. He kissed me back, but there was a hint of uncertainty in his eyes, which I hated to see there. I gave him a smiley peck on his lips until he smiled back, and I threaded our fingers. He slid over a little closer on the couch.

Kell came back out with two bottles of water and handed us one each, then disappeared back into the kitchen. "So how was Uncle Clydey today?" she called out.

I finally managed to look away from Merrick. "Uh, he was . . . I don't know. Clyde was weird today."

Kell sat on the couch opposite us and tucked her foot up, her glass of lemon soda in hand. "What do you mean?"

"I don't know. It's hard to describe. He said he was fine, but he wasn't *as* grumpy . . . well, he's always grumpy, but he was more secretive." I shrugged and looked back at Merrick. "I did get him to admit that he and your Uncle Donny are kind of dating, but not dating. I dunno. He was weird about it."

Merrick's eyebrows rose. "Dating?"

"I think so. But honestly, every conversation I had with him today was weird." No way was I mentioning the purchase of lube.

"Should you be worried?" Kell asked.

"About what? The weirdness? Or the dating?" I asked. "He still told me to shut up and to mind my own business and to quit my stupid worrying, so he's fine."

Kell nodded seriously. "Well, that's a relief."

"Uncle Donny was weird today too," Merrick added. "I called him this afternoon and he said he was going away for a few days, which is not like him at all."

"Did he say where?"

"No." Merrick frowned. "I asked him if he wanted me to mind Lulu, his crazy bird, but he said no."

"His bird?" I asked, and the penny dropped. "Um, Clyde bought birdseed today."

Merrick stared at me. "He did?"

I nodded. "Holy shit. Is Clyde bird-sitting Lulu?"

Merrick burst out laughing. "I have no idea."

I checked my watch. "It's too late to call him now. He goes to bed with the sun." I shot Merrick a look. "I might drop in unannounced to see him tomorrow after work. If I take an apple teacake, he'll be happy to see me."

He squeezed my hand. "I could come with you. I'll be able to tell you if it's Lulu or not."

"Sure," I agreed. "But I can't be held responsible for

anything Clyde says. If you think he can be brutal in public, you just wait till you see him in his natural habitat."

Merrick laughed. "I'm sure it'll be fine."

"Oh, Clydey is a big ol' softie," Kell said. "You just need to know how to handle him.

I snorted. "Tell Merrick about the time you first met Clyde."

"Well, first time I met Clyde," Kell said, "we were at the Arcus centre and he just came right out and asked me how many lesbians it took to change a lightbulb. I said one, because we get shit done, and he laughed so hard he cried."

"And Clyde then proceeded to tell me," I furthered, "that he liked Kell more than he liked me. And for a gay man, that was saying something."

Merrick laughed. "That's a classic."

Kell's phone rang. She held it up to show me the screen. Selena was calling. "Eeek! I'm gonna go take this in my room. Merrick, it was really nice to meet you!" she said, grinning and waving as she walked to the hall, and we heard her answer the call. "Hello, beautiful," she said before her bedroom door closed.

I sighed. "Things with Selena are very new. She's crushed on her for ages, so she's all excited."

"I really like Kell," Merrick said warmly. "She's great. I can see why you get on so well."

"She likes you," I replied.

"She does?"

"Yeah, because she didn't grill you on . . . well, everything. Like a terrorist interrogator."

"Would she really have done that?"

"Maybe. But she knows how much I like you, so maybe not." My brain went offline for a stupid second, and I froze. Did I just say that out loud? *Yep. Pretty sure I did.*

"I really like you too," Merrick replied. "And I'd very much like to kiss you right now. I've wanted to kiss you all night."

My whole body went warm all over. I nodded, and he leaned in close and ghosted his lips over mine. "Should we take this into your room?"

I nodded. "Yeah." I took his hand and led him into my room, and I walked straight to my bedside table and turned the lamp on. Merrick hit the light switch so the only light was the soft glow of the lamp, and he closed the door. He leaned against it and I turned to face him. I could see a bulge in his jeans and I swallowed hard.

Christ.

He strode toward me and took hold of my face, bringing me in for a hard kiss. His mouth opened mine and he gave me his tongue, all while holding my face to his.

My knees almost gave out, and with the sudden rush of blood from my brain to my groin, I was surprised I didn't fall over. Or was he holding me up? I was too lightheaded to care. Without breaking the kiss, he pushed me onto the bed and crawled on top of me, pressing his weight onto me.

I groaned like a wannabe porn star.

I loved being manhandled in bed. I loved it when a guy took charge and manoeuvred me how he wanted. I loved it when the top took charge. And Merrick did it all so well.

I had no doubt when, or if, he did eventually fuck me, it was going to be incredible.

We frantically undid each other's jeans and I wrapped my hand around his erection. He was rock-hard and burning hot, and he gasped and bucked into my hand. I thought he was going to come but he didn't. The smell of sex clung to us, and I wanted it. So bad. "God, you feel so good," he murmured into my mouth.

His hand felt amazing but I wanted more. "I want to taste you," I ground out.

He stilled, and I wondered if it was too much, but he pulled back. His lips were swollen and wet, his eyes dark. "What a good idea," he whispered. He got to his knees, then shuffled up a bit, lying back down on his side.

I quickly got the idea and rolled toward him. It took a little rearranging and a bit of wiggling, but we made it work. Smiling, I licked the head of his cock just when he sucked me into his hot, wet mouth. I almost came right then.

At least having his dick in my face, in my mouth, down my throat, was a good distraction.

We still had our jeans on, so it was kind of confining and a bit awkward, but holy hell, it was so, so good.

He thrust into my mouth and gripped my hip, groaning as I sucked him. I could tell he was close. He was swollen and leaking precome; his thrusts had fallen out of rhythm.

He pulled off my cock. "Leo," he moaned. "I'm gonna . . ."

I hummed around him and made no attempt to pull away, and he came, shooting down my throat. He gave a strangled cry before he sucked me back into his mouth. He was still convulsing with his orgasm when I gave him mine.

Sometime later, when the world had stopped spinning, we were lying on my bed in each other's arms. I had my head on his chest and he rubbed my back, kissing my forehead every now and then.

"I should get going home," he said. "I have an early class, and you have to work."

"Hmm. I know."

"What was it that you wanted to talk about?" he asked. "Earlier, you said you wanted to talk."

I leaned up on my hand. "It was nothing, really. Clyde

had me weirded out and my brain went into overdrive. He just said something that . . ." I sighed. "It's nothing. He got all bent out of shape not knowing the full details of our relationship, but then he's bird-sitting your uncle's bird and he doesn't tell me."

"He wanted to know the full details of our relationship?"

"Well, not exactly. He was just lecturing me on mutual respect when he can't even tell me the truth." I frowned. "I think he was projecting. I don't know. I will call around and see him tomorrow, though, and maybe give him some of his own medicine."

Merrick traced my eyebrow and looked me in the eye. "You sure you're okay?"

I nodded. "Yep. I'm very happy with how things are between you and me. I know I wanted to push things earlier, like a sex-maniac hooker, but honestly, I'm glad we didn't. What we have is perfect just as it is." I thumbed his jaw, feeling the stubble there, and smiling. "Clyde's just stuck in the sixties and seventies when everything was a secret and gay people didn't have, couldn't have, didn't want romance. He doesn't understand." I sighed again. "Or maybe it's because he has had to hide everything about his true self for his entire life and that's why he doesn't understand. I shouldn't be so harsh on him. We grew up in different times. It's not his fault he's a miserable git."

Merrick smiled. "You're a good man, Leo. You have a good heart."

I took his hand and held it to my chest, letting him feel the thumping rhythm under my skin. "Right now I have a very happy heart."

He gasped and rolled me over for a kiss so he was on top of me again. "So do I."

CHAPTER SIXTEEN

MERRICK

LEAVING Leo's place was one of the hardest things I've ever had to do. I wanted to crawl into bed with him, I wanted to be naked, and I wanted to make love to him. I wanted to bury myself inside him, to become part of him. And I wanted to stay there, possibly forever.

Instead, I crawled into my bed, very much alone.

I stared at the ceiling for far too long, and I came to the conclusion of what I'd been fighting for three weeks. And now, in hindsight, I wondered why I'd implemented such a stupid rule.

Leo and I were good. We were good together, and yeah, maybe holding out for a few dates was the sensible thing to do. Maybe it did put us on a solid foundation . . . Or maybe I was scared to put myself out there. Maybe I was afraid of putting my heart on the line until I was sure he wouldn't hurt me. My every waking moment for the last five years had been my work, my business. I was so driven to see it succeed, I hadn't even looked twice at another guy.

But Leo walked into my studio and into my life, into my heart. He was a genuine guy, no pretences, no charades. He wouldn't hurt me deliberately. He wouldn't ask me to choose between him and my work. He knew how important my studio was to me.

Leo wouldn't break my heart. Not intentionally. And I certainly wouldn't hurt him. I truly thought he and I could be something long-term. I was thinking long-term, anyway, and I was certain he was too. I remembered the way he'd put my hand on his chest and told me his heart was happy, and my heart bloomed with warmth.

I rolled over and took my phone off the bedside table. It was almost two in the morning, so he probably wouldn't read any messages until he woke up, but I needed to say this.

Leo, I can't sleep. Just wanted you to know I really regret leaving your place tonight. I wish I was still in your bed, and I really wish I hadn't imposed that stupid rule. WTF was I even thinking? I know you said you're happy with things as they are, and I am too. But I'm also ready to take the next step when you are.

It wasn't eloquent and not even remotely romantic, but I needed him to know. I hit Send before I could change my mind, slid my phone onto its charging pad, and with a smile, closed my eyes.

MY PHONE BEEPED, waking me up at half six. I hadn't slept anywhere near enough. My phone beeped again, and I grumbled as I reached for it. Until I saw Leo's name. My heart skipped a beat, and I grinned as I read his reply.

Good morning, Mr Bowman. Sorry you couldn't sleep. I know a remedy for that. Perhaps if you'd phoned me at 2am instead of texting, I could have made a house call to administer it myself.

I laughed just as another text came through.

Leo the tiny lion says hi.

Followed by a photograph of the little ceramic lion I'd given him sitting on his bedside table.

Tell Leo the tiny lion I said hi.

Then I quickly sent another. *It's perfectly natural to be jealous of a little tiny lion, right?*

I waited for his reply, but my phone rang instead. It was Leo. "Jealous?"

"Good morning to you too," I said. My voice croaked from sleep.

"Oh yes, good morning to you too," he said lightly. I could tell he was smiling.

"Yes, I am jealous of the tiny little lion that is beside you right now. It should have been me."

He hummed. "Should have been. But you took the moral high-ground and . . ." He gasped. "Oh my God, are you trying to protect my virtue? Because I squandered my virtue away when I was seventeen."

"Seventeen? You began early."

"Yep. Seventeen, horny, and stupid."

I snorted. "I was nineteen," I admitted. "I had no clue what I was doing. Thank God for the internet for gay sex education, that's all I'm saying."

He laughed, warm in my ear. "Ain't that the truth. Though the internet is also responsible for my being able to watch *Queer as Folk* a hundred times and, therefore, completely to blame for my unrealistic expectations of what the perfect guy is."

"Who was your favourite?"

"Oh my God, Brian. When I was younger, I had delusions of grandeur that I would be just like Brian, and all I wanted in a boyfriend was my very own Brian. But now I'm older and somewhat wiser, I realise that Brian was actually a jerk and I'm more of a Justin. Or an Emmett."

That made me smile. "Brian was a bit of a jerk. But damn, he was hot."

"Hell yes, he was. Which character would you be?"

"Hmm," I considered this. "I'm not sure. A little bit Justin because he's an artist. A little bit Brian because he's driven by work and he's bossy, but mostly I'm just Debbie."

"Mikey's mum?"

I laughed. "Yep. The voice of reason and has terrible dress sense."

He chuckled. "There's nothing wrong with your dress sense. It's sexy as fuck."

"Sexy . . . ?" I snorted. That was ridiculous.

"Hell yes. It's totally a relaxed-businessman, talented-and-confident look, and I happen to find it sexy as hell."

I laughed again, my chest warming at his compliment. "Thanks, I guess."

Leo was quiet a moment. "Sorry you couldn't sleep last night."

I scrubbed my hand over my face. "I was just . . . over-thinking."

"Hey, overthinking is my niche. Find your own."

I smiled again but let out another sigh. "I shouldn't have left last night. I shouldn't have imposed that stupid rule."

"Yes, you should have."

"What?"

"It was a comfort thing and a boundaries thing. And even as much as I didn't like it at first, I can respect why you did it. You needed to feel comfortable with me before we did that, and that's fine. You don't need to apologise. I'd rather you were honest with me than regret it later." He sighed. "The thing is, Merrick, if you'd decided that you never wanted to have anal sex, ever, I'd be okay with that. Everything else we've done is . . . well, it's amazing, and I don't want you to feel pressured about anything."

His words felt like a blanket around me. "I do want to. But thank you for saying that and for being so understanding. Some guys probably wouldn't be."

"Can I tell you something?"

"Sure."

"At first I thought it was about me, and I wondered if maybe you weren't interested in me. But then I realised it wasn't about me. I mean, who knew I was not the centre of the universe, right?" I snorted and he continued, "Anyway, so once I came to grips with the entire world not revolving around me, I realised your decision was about you and about comfort and consent. You needed this, and what kind of arsehole would I be if I forced you into something you weren't entirely comfortable with?"

I wasn't sure what to say to that. God, there was so much I wanted to say. I settled on, "You're definitely not an arsehole."

"Well, I can be," he replied. "Just eat all the purple Skittles and see how you like me then."

I burst out laughing. "Duly noted. And the blue peanut M&M's, right?"

"Correct."

"Anyway, after I had to defend our decision to Clyde, I realised you were right. We were right to put down some boundaries."

"You had to defend me to Clyde?" I was a little stunned. "Um . . ."

"No, not you," he said quickly. "Just the waiting thing.

He didn't get it. He was all 'back in my day . . .' and I had to explain to him that we're not like that. You and me. We made the decision to wait and it was none of his business."

"Well, *I* made that decision . . ."

"Yeah, and *I* agreed to it. Because I respect you. And anyway, it's not like we're both virgins who are saving ourselves for marriage or whatever. And even if we were, it'd still be none of Clyde's business." He swallowed hard. "And I told you at first I was a bit hurt, but Kell kinda pointed out that it really must be awful to have someone who wants to respect me instead of use me, so that was a bit of a reality check. I guess I'm used to guys just wanting one thing, and when you didn't, I didn't know what to make of that."

"So Kell was the voice of reason."

"Kell's always my voice of reason. She's like the angel that sit on my shoulder. Always offering sage advice and a kind word, unless she's had a bottle of wine too many; then she becomes the little devil on my other shoulder and we end up getting cautioned by the cops for shenanigans in public."

I laughed. "I can see that."

"It was all her idea, officer."

Now I was smiling at my ceiling like a crazy man. God, I really liked him. He did things to my heart and my belly that I hadn't experienced in a long time. It was all erratic thumping and butterflies. "I don't want to wait anymore," I said quietly. "So when the time's right and you want to . . ."

I heard him swallow. "Um, sure. That's good to know." He let out a long breath. "That's um . . . duly noted." Then he cleared his throat. "Goddammit. Now I'm gonna be thinking about that all day."

I laughed, breathily. "Same."

"So I was gonna go see Clyde this afternoon . . ."

"I can still go with you if you want?"

"I want."

"Then afterwards we could grab some dinner," I added, hoping it might lead to something else.

He made a sound in the back of his throat that told me he was definitely on the same page. "Uh, yeah, that sounds great." There was a rustling noise. Was that his bed covers? "Okay, so now I can't stop the mental porn show in my head. I need to go jerk off in the shower if I intend to make it to work on time."

I laughed, but my dick ached. "If it's any consolation, I'm gonna go do the same. Think of me while you do it."

"You son of a bitch," he whispered. "Now I have to walk out in the hall with a boner."

I laughed again. "See you this afternoon. I'll pick you up around six, yeah?"

"Yeah," he groaned. "If I'm not arrested for indecency because I'll be sporting a hard-on all day, but sure. Six o'clock sounds great."

He clicked off the call and I laughed, the sound echoing around my loft. Then I threw back the covers and headed for the shower to do exactly what I hoped Leo was doing in his shower. Was sex by proxy even a thing? By the time I got under the hot water, I didn't care. Knowing there was a very good chance I was going to be inside him tonight, imagining it, picturing it, how he would feel, the sounds he would make . . . I came twice.

"LOOK AT YOUR SMILE," Ciara said, handing me a coffee. Pretty sure her grin matched mine. We weren't open yet; I'd finished checking my stock quantities of different clay, glazes, and oxides, and Ciara was filling the cake fridge.

I tried to rein it in but eventually just laughed. "I'm just happy, that's all."

"And I'm sure a certain cutie named Leo has nothing to do with that."

"Maybe he does." My stupid face told her he most definitely did. "Things are going very well."

"I'm happy for you."

"Please don't say it's about time."

"It's about time."

"Thanks."

She laughed. "Busy day today," she said, restocking the milk fridge. "You've got two full sessions, and I've got Hoshi coming in to help me with the morning rush. She'll be here in a few minutes."

"Excellent." And yes, two full sessions at the wheel today was exactly what I needed. "I need to be done by five at the latest."

"Hot date tonight?"

"Yep." I smirked behind my coffee. "Well, hopefully."

She laughed again. "Ready for me to open the doors?"

"Sure am. Class starts in half an hour." There were already joggers and dog walkers waiting outside. "And you've already got your first customers."

Ciara opened the door and the customers filed in; Hoshi was one of them. "Morning," she said brightly, fixing her apron.

I left them to it and got ready for my day, knowing I always had some early arrivers for my Saturday morning class. And sure enough, the first two came in ten minutes later just as I was bringing out the new clays for today.

"Morning!" Johanna said brightly. "I've been looking forward to today."

"We both have," Gary added. "Such a highlight of our week."

I grinned at them. "Thank you. I love hearing that. Saturday morning class is a highlight of my week too."

Gary and Johanna were a married couple who had been coming every Saturday for almost three years, and I really enjoyed their company.

"Have we got the Ironstone today?" Johanna asked.

"We most certainly do. Delivered yesterday," I replied and her grin widened. "You're doing your third piece today, is that right?" They were actually a set of canisters for her kids. She and Gary had three adult kids, and the first year, she made them each a set of coffee mugs. Second year, she made them all serving platter sets, and this year it was a set of canisters for flour, sugar, coffee, and tea. Each set was designed specifically for that child, and each year, they apparently loved their gifts. She really was improving each year, and these canister sets were going to be gorgeous.

"Yes!" She clapped her hands together. "Can't wait."

Gary preferred to hand-build, though he did enjoy his time at the wheel. But Gary, he just loved to sit at the workbench and create small pots, figurines, tealight holders, vases, pen holders . . . whatever took his fancy. He had a great eye for detail and his work was intricate, but his sense of humour showed through.

And that's what I loved about pottery. It was so individual, so personal. It could be as big or small as you wanted. It could be functional and practical or simply bring you joy to look at.

"What are you working on today?" Gary asked.

"I was really looking forward to spending some time at

the wheel today," I admitted. "Just getting lost in it, ya know?"

He gave me a happy nod. "Can't wait to see what you turn out. Love those crackle-glaze bowls in the café you made. I might try that this time."

"Awesome," I replied.

More of the class soon arrived, and in no time, we were all up to our elbows in clay. Some of us quite literally. This class was advanced enough that I didn't need to stand by and assist or guide. It had almost become a group of friends having a potter's session, so I wasn't lying when I said it was a highlight for me. Saturday morning classes were where I threw some of my best work, and most of the items for sale in the café were born from my time in this class.

I sat at my wheel and got lost in the rhythmic hum and how the clay turned in my hand. It was almost like a metronome for me, a perfect tempo, relaxing in its rhythm. There was something about taking a lump of clay and making it malleable in my hands, turning it into something beautiful.

By the end of the session, I had four huge, deep round bowls, and four sets of salad servers. Smooth, wide, and flat-ish, and I was thinking maybe a plum-and-onyx mirror glaze for one set, an obsidian turquoise for another. A black-and-white set, and maybe a matte grey set . . .

I had a few weeks to decide on colours and finishes yet, so into the drying room they went along with everyone else's. And when the class was over, I waved everyone off and cleaned up, grabbing a bite to eat, then prepped for the next class.

This next class was up to the glazing stage of their pieces, so we all got to sit around the work table and chatter away. I finished off dog and cat bowls, which sold surprisingly well, and helped around the room as needed, and before I knew it, it was four-thirty and I was cleaning up.

I had one hour to mop the floors, then get myself showered and dressed and out the door, which was plenty of time. Fifty minutes later, the café had closed, the doors were locked, and the Closed sign was up. I set the alarm and I walked to my car. I told myself my smile wasn't just because I was going to see Leo, but because this was proof that I could have both: a business and a relationship.

I'd spent the last five years avoiding any distraction. I was focused and driven; my only goal was to be successful. But maybe my brother was right; I could have both. Maybe not in the beginning, when I needed to be focussed. But now that I was established and everything ran smoothly, I could make room in my life for someone else.

Leo had come into my life with perfect timing. Perfect finesse, perfect humour, a perfect heart. I was really trying not to get ahead of myself, but it was almost certainly too late.

I was falling for him, hard and fast.

It should have scared me, or at least made me question if it was because it'd been so long since I'd spent time with anyone. But I was ready to just freefall. Leap without looking, jump in with both feet, dive in headfirst, and whatever other cheesy metaphor I could think of. I just wanted to grab whatever happiness I could get with both hands.

And as foolish as that might have been, a voice in the back of my mind told me it was because, perhaps on some crazy level, I was thinking Leo could maybe be the one.

The *one*.

And that thought knocked the wind out of me. I didn't know whether to laugh or puke.

The car behind me honked its horn, startling the crap

out of me. I hadn't noticed the lights change, but I drove on, thankful for the distraction. But by the time I got to Leo's place, my heart was racing and my belly was in knots. I was so damn excited to see him, so nervous about how this night might end. If we did end up in bed, it was likely to be over way too fast.

I was just about a nervous wreck when I got to his door. But there he was, freshly showered and grinning at me like he felt the exact same as me. A waft of his scent hit me; his smile undid everything inside me. My nerves were gone, replaced with only surety that, yes, my heart knew exactly what it was doing.

"Hey," he whispered.

"Hey," I replied.

He seemed to recoup the ability to speak first. He opened the door further. "Come in. Just gotta put my shoes on."

As I stepped inside, he closed the door and brushed his lips to mine. My breath caught and my stomach flipped. He smelt so good. He tasted even better.

"Hi, Merrick," Kell said from somewhere in the flat. "Did Leo even let you get through the door first?"

"Yes," Leo answered. He took my hand and led me into the living room. "I have some manners."

"Hi, Kell," I answered.

"You two are so cute," she said, rolling her eyes. Then she held up a dress in each hand: one peacock blue, one a rather bright orange. "I can't decide. Which one?"

Leo and I answered in unison. "Blue."

We grinned at each other and Kell sighed. "Blue it is. But I wanted to wear my white heels . . ."

Then Leo added, "Honey, no. Not unless you want to

be Smurfette. Wear the blue dress with your little black cardi, black heels, black clutch."

"You just hate those white high heels."

"True. I told you that when you bought them."

"No, you said they were a bold choice."

"Which is gay for 'honey, no.'"

She sighed dramatically. "Well, you need to start speaking lesbian."

"I'll try and remember that."

She looked at us both. "Are you heading out now?"

"Yep, we'll go see Clyde first, then grab some dinner?" he replied, but looking at me.

"Sounds good."

"Well," Kell added. "Merrick, I hope to see you again in the morning." She then shot Leo a knowing look. "Have fun."

Leo blushed at how she implied I'd be spending the night. "Thanks, Kell. And I hope Selena is here in the morning so I can embarrass you in front of her."

She grinned as she walked down the hall, holding her blue dress like a flag. "Oh, and if you hear any loud moaning coming from my room, no need to call Ghostbusters."

Her door clicked behind her and Leo sighed. "That's a visual I wasn't exactly prepared for."

I laughed. "You two are so great together."

He grinned at me. "Did you have a good day?"

"I had a great day! It helps when I have the best job in the world."

He was smiling at me as if he was simply happy that I was happy. He pecked his lips to mine. "You ready to go?"

I nodded. "Sure am."

He gave himself the wallet/phone/keys pat down, then

pulled on his shoes. "Let's go and see what Clyde's really up to."

NOW THERE'S a lot to be said about the element of surprise. On one hand, the surpris*er* gets to see the surpris*ee* in their element. If they'd be questioning unusual behaviour, then perhaps they would get the answer they sought.

On the other hand, the surpris*ers*—in this case, Leo and I—were the ones to be surprised.

Because Clyde opened the door, looking every part as normal as I'd ever seen him. He wore comfy house clothes and had his cane in one hand. But when he saw it was us, the smile died right off his face.

And behind him came a familiar voice. "Is that dinner?" Uncle Donny asked as he came into view with a flourish. But it was Uncle Donny like I'd never seen him. He wore a floral silk dressing gown with pink feather trim and tiny, fluffy pink heels.

If we'd been going for the element of surprise, we were not disappointed.

CHAPTER SEVENTEEN

LEO

OKAY, that wasn't what I'd been expecting at all, and so much happened so fast. Clyde stepped in front of Donny, not so much to block our view but more in a protective manner. Donny's expression was horrified, and Clyde's . . . Well, Clyde's was more heartbreak than I could stand.

He began to close the door, but I stopped him. I couldn't let him close the door because it seemed so final. I didn't want to end our friendship like this because would he ever want to see me after this? "Clyde, wait. Wait, please."

"What do you want?" he barked. "You ain't ever heard of calling first? What the hell is wrong with you, boy? You can't just be turning up on someone's doorstep unannounced."

"I was worried," I said, which wasn't a complete lie. His brows knitted together like my words caused him pain. "Please, let us come in."

He looked over his shoulder, and though we couldn't see Donny's response, Clyde stood back and opened the door. We stepped inside, just in time to see Donny tighten the robe around himself and slowly sit on the couch. He toed out of his heels, his face a mask of sadness.

"Oh no," Merrick said, rushing to his uncle's side. Clyde reached out to stop Merrick, but I put my hand on Clyde's arm. I knew Merrick would do the right thing. He sat right next to his uncle, his arm around Donny's back. "Leave them on."

Donny shook his head, his voice just a whisper. "You weren't ever supposed to see this."

"Why?" Merrick asked gently. "If it's who you are, then I want to see. I want to know the real you. There's no shame here."

Donny looked at Merrick then, his eyes full of tears. "You don't mind?"

Merrick shook his head. "Not at all. I'm just sorry you couldn't tell me sooner."

Donny began to cry a little, and Merrick hugged him. Clyde gave me a nod. "I better make some tea."

Clyde and I ducked into the small kitchen while Merrick and his uncle talked. It was hard to give them complete privacy when Clyde's unit was so small. He filled the kettle and flipped the button, then set about measuring out the loose-leaf tea into the pot. It certainly explained him buying the tea. I leaned back to check the balcony and, sure enough, there was a birdcage.

"You could have told me he was coming over this weekend," I said quietly.

"It wasn't a secret for my benefit," he murmured. "Donny . . . he ain't ever told anyone but me that he . . ." He glanced to where Donny and Merrick were talking. "He thought he was safe here to be himself."

"He is safe here," I said. "Merrick loves him. He just wants him to be happy."

Clyde gave me a dark look. "We come from a different generation, Leo. Back when we were your age, everything was behind closed doors. It had to be a secret unless you wanted to risk being arrested or bashed. I know that still happens nowadays, but not as much. At least who we are is not illegal now."

My heart squeezed. "I know. And I'm sorry. I don't mean to sound so flippant. I'm not dismissing what you went through. I'm just saying that my generation is okay with this. And we're only okay with it because your generation put in the hard yards first."

He gave a sad nod. "He was just going to stay this weekend. Wear what he wanted, be whoever he wanted to be."

"Be himself," I added.

Clyde nodded. "Yep."

"Clyde, I'm really proud of you. You're the first person he's ever felt comfortable with, and that's amazing."

He blustered a bit. "Yeah, well. I'm not the one who's amazing." His gaze went back to Donny. He didn't have to say anything else. I could see it on his face.

I squeezed his shoulder just as the kettle boiled and clicked itself off. "Let's get this tea made."

Clyde produced a tray I'd never seen before. I was pretty sure it was a genuine 1960s piece that people would pay good money for these days. Clyde fixed four teacups and some sugar and milk in a little jug, which he'd never done for me before. He was being all fancy for Donny, and it made me so happy for him.

I carried the tray out and slid it onto the coffee table in front of Merrick and Donny. Donny let go of Merrick's hand so he could pour the tea, and when Merrick looked up at me, he smiled so beautifully. It made my heart do a full swoop, and I gave him a pointed look that asked if he was okay. He gave a small nod in return.

"So," Donny said. He sat with perfect posture, proud. "To clear the air . . . I just want to say that, while I appreciate how some women's clothing feels, I'm not . . . I don't wish to be . . . I'm very happy being a man. I just also happen to like to dress up occasionally, that's all. Before you go thinking anything, I would like to clarify that. And although some days I feel more feminine than masculine, I know that I am a man."

"You don't have to clarify anything," Merrick said. "Or justify anything.

"Donny," I began gently. "There is absolutely nothing wrong at all with being gender-fluid or non-binary. A lot of people are, and it's one hundred per cent okay."

"I already told him that," Clyde grumbled at me. I turned to stare at him, surprised. "What?" he barked. "You don't think I listen to those folks at the Arcus Centre? Christ, Leo. How long have we been going?"

I got a little teary. "Oh my God, Clyde. I'm so proud of you!"

He rolled his eyes and sighed. My comment or reaction was clearly not getting a response.

Merrick smiled at me, then patted Donny's knee. "See? Like I said. It's okay. If you want to wear a pretty dress, then wear it. Or if you feel like wearing trousers, then wear them. It doesn't matter to me, just as long as you're happy."

Donny got a little teary again and he tightened his gown around himself. He looked directly at Clyde. "Clyde was the first person I told, and he was very kind." Clyde blushed, and I nudged him so hard he almost spilled his tea. "I never realised how much it meant to not have to hide this part of me."

Merrick put his tea down and took Donny's hand again. "You don't have to hide anymore."

"I think I would like to learn more about this gender-fluid or non-binary thing," Donny said, sniffling a little. "Maybe it might make some sense."

"I can take you," Merrick offered. "To the centre that Leo and Clyde go to. Anytime you like. I can take both you and Clyde, and Leo too. We can all go. You and Clyde can speak to someone there, and Leo can show me around. I've been meaning to go."

Donny let out a huge sigh and wiped at his eye. His chin wobbled. "I've had to hide this away my whole life." He breathed in a shaky breath. "I don't know what to think now you know, Merrick. I can't undo this."

Merrick put his arm around Donny's shoulder. "You don't have to undo it. And this can be just between you and me, forever. No one else needs to know. But you can be open with me, and honest. Hell, I'll take you shopping at Victoria's Secret if you want. I don't care what anyone else thinks. Uncle Donny, I care what you think and how you feel."

Donny gave him a teary smile. "Thank you, Merrick. That means a lot."

"Donny," I said. "I don't know if you know this or not, but a lot of the gender-fluid folks will wear a different coloured bracelet, depending on how they feel that day. One day, they might wear blue, the next day it might be the pink bracelet. Or green and purple, or whatever colour code you like. That way, no one else has to know anything but the people closest to you will know how you feel that day without you having to say a word. So you might have to go out somewhere but don't feel comfortable wearing something feminine in public, but if you wear your coloured bracelet that day, *we'll* know how you're feeling, and *we* can be a little more gentle with you that day. Or get you home again if you need to bail." I shrugged. "It's just an idea."

Donny's eyes welled with more tears, and to my surprise, so did Merrick's. "That's a really good idea," Merrick said. Then he looked back to his uncle. "I can get those for you. You just tell me which colours."

I could feel Clyde's eyes on me, and I turned to find him smiling. There was a knock at the door. "Oh, that'll be dinner," Clyde said.

"I'll get it," I said, jumping up and going to the door. They'd ordered Chinese food, so I took it straight to the table and collected two dinner plates and some cutlery.

"Okay, we'll let you two have dinner," Merrick said, standing. It seemed like it was a conversation cut short, but perhaps Donny needed some space to get his head around what had happened. Perhaps Merrick did too.

Clyde winched himself up with his walking stick, and Donny stood to help him. He'd slipped his pink fluffy heels back on and tied off his slinky gown. He looked emotional still, but as though an almighty weight had been lifted off his shoulders.

Merrick gave him a hug, and when he looked at Clyde as if to hug him too, Clyde held up his walking stick like a sword. Merrick put his hands up in surrender and I snorted out a laugh. "I'll take that hug," I said, holding out my arms, and Merrick walked straight into them. When he buried his face into my neck and held me a little tighter, I knew he needed the hug more than me.

"Okay, we're gonna go," I declared.

Clyde sat himself down at the dining table and Donny walked out of the kitchen holding a pitcher of iced water.

He really did look fantastic. "Donny," I said with a smile. "Those heels do great things for your legs."

Clyde shot me a dirty look. "Keep your eyes on your own prize, thanks very much. And leave mine alone."

Donny giggled and swatted at Clyde, but then his face softened. "Thank you, Leo. And Merrick, I'll call you. But thank you, too."

"Call me, anytime," he replied.

We left them to it and walked to the car in silence. We didn't get in the car; we leaned against it and let what had just happened settle over us. "Well," Merrick said eventually. "That was not what I was expecting."

I chuckled. "Uh, no. Me either."

He ran both hands through his hair. "I had no idea." He looked at me, bewildered. "I'm just . . . stunned."

"You were so great in there," I said. "Everything you said was exactly what he needed to hear."

Merrick's eyes were wide. "I've never seen him so . . . happy. I don't know if that's the right word. Free . . . No, that's not— Yeah, maybe free."

"He seemed lighter," I offered. "Like the two times I've seen him at the studio, he seemed burdened. And just now, it was like he wasn't carrying that burden anymore."

Merrick met my gaze and nodded. "Yes." He let out a shaky breath. "Christ. Imagine being seventy years old and only just being free to be yourself." He shook his head in disbelief. "I can't imagine that. We're lucky, aren't we? That we live in a day and age where we have information and support communities. I mean, I know not everyone does, and I'm very lucky that my family are fine with me being gay. I know Kell didn't have that luxury, and I'm sorry. That must have been so awful. I can't even imagine. And now she has you and your family. But for seventy years, Uncle

Donny never had that. He never had anyone. He lived in fear. Miserable. He was *miserable,* Leo. For seventy years. He didn't even have a name for what he feels." Merrick put his hand to his forehead. "Sorry, I'm just rambling."

"Hey, don't be sorry," I said, pulling him in for a hug. He clung to me. "I get it. Yes, we're lucky compared to what they lived through. Guys like Clyde paved the way for us, and I'm thankful. But Merrick, your uncle Donny doesn't have to be miserable anymore."

He pulled back and searched my eyes. "I want to help him, as much as I can."

I held his face and kissed him. "Me too."

"Did you see his gown? Did you see how fucking gorgeous that was?"

I laughed. "Yes. Was it Japanese silk? It looked hella expensive."

"I have no idea. I think I need to take him shopping. There are plenty of ambiguous clothing lines these days that could suit him for everyday wear. You know those long shirt type things that look like a dress but the men can wear pants? I think they're linen. I don't know what to call them."

I chuckled at how excited he was. "But we can find out."

He nodded. "Maybe he'd feel more comfortable in a Japanese *haori* and *hakama.* The traditional shirt and skirt for men. I don't know . . . maybe he'll just want to go to the dress section at Target." He sighed skyward and shook his head. "Whatever he wants is fine, right?"

"Right."

"And those shoes." He made a face. "Pink fluffy ones are fine for at home, but they'll kill his feet if he tries to go to the supermarket in them. Maybe I can convince him to get some ballet flats."

I burst out laughing and kissed him again. "Slow down. He might need a few days to deal with the fact that now three people know his secret."

Merrick looked me right in the eyes. "I don't want him to have to wait another day. He's waited seventy years, Leo."

My heart squeezed and I put my forehead to his. "You're kind of great, you know that?"

He put his hands around my waist, inhaled deeply, and closed his eyes. "So are you. Thank you for suggesting the bracelet thing. That's a really good idea."

"No problem at all."

He buried his face against my neck, and after a long, quiet moment, he hummed. "Should we go find food? Are you hungry?"

"I'm always hungry."

"Dine out or order in?"

I smiled against the side of his head. "Uh, can we eat first? Because let's be real, if we go back to your place or mine, there won't be any food ordered or eaten."

He chuckled. "True."

"But whatever we decide, can we make it quick? Because you had an epiphany at two o'clock this morning that I'd really like to see it through before you change your mind."

His whole body shook with his laughter. "Yes, I did. But believe me," he said, pulling back to kiss me on the lips, "I'm not changing my mind. I want to take you to bed and do everything you want me to do to you."

Christ. My knees almost gave out and my blood ran hot. "Okay then. McDonald's drive-thru it is. This is gonna be the quickest dinner ever."

Merrick burst out laughing again, but he opened the passenger door for me. "Your McChariot awaits."

WE DIDN'T GET McDonald's. We found a parking spot right out front a pizzeria that Merrick swore had slices in a display oven, ready to go. And thankfully, they did. We ordered and were served within a few minutes, and it was so much better than Maccas. It also gave Merrick some more time to process what we'd just discovered.

"How are you feeling about everything now?" I asked.

"With Uncle Donny?" he clarified, to which I nodded. "Um, sad, to be honest."

"Sad? Why sad?"

"Because he's lived his whole life behind closed doors. He's always been quiet and shied away from people. I just thought that was him, ya know? But now I have to wonder if it was because he never felt comfortable, and that's just sad. I hate that I didn't know earlier. I should have realised sooner."

"He wasn't ready before," I offered.

"But he told Clyde, and he's known him for two weeks," Merrick admitted with a frown. "I know that shouldn't bother me, but I just keep thinking back and wondering if I missed something. Could I have done better?"

I reached over and took his hand. "There's a really good chance he never let on because he didn't want to lose you. You're too important to him, and he had more to risk by telling you. Telling Clyde, a virtual stranger, was so much easier because he had nothing to lose."

Merrick threaded our fingers and met my gaze. "You're good at knowing what to say."

"And you're good at match-making," I said. "You met Clyde once and knew he and your uncle would get on."

"I didn't expect them to get on that well. I thought they

could be friends. Uncle Donny's always liked forthright people." He sipped his drink.

"I think he likes having a daddy."

Merrick snorted water out his nose, laughing as he quickly dabbed serviettes to his face and down his shirt.

"Clyde also bought lube at the supermarket. I wasn't going to tell you," I added.

Merrick coughed and spluttered. "Stop it!"

"To be fair, when he bought it, I wasn't one hundred per cent sure if it was for his personal use or with someone else."

Merrick was still laughing. "I don't know whether to be horrified or proud."

"I'm a little proud, not gonna lie."

Merrick grinned, and he just stared at me for a long moment. "Thank you."

"What for?"

"For . . ." His smile faltered, but he held my gaze. "For coming into my life when you did. For being yourself. For wanting to spend time with me. For giving me those nervous butterflies that I was certain, up until three weeks ago, were utter bullshit. For making me smile, for making me laugh. For helping me see the real Uncle Donny, because if I hadn't met you, I'm sure he'd still be lonely and hiding his true self."

Oh.

Holy shit.

I couldn't seem to string a coherent thought. My heart was banging around in my chest so hard it almost hurt. "Wow."

"Was that too much?" he asked, his cheeks red.

"Oh, no, Goldilocks, that was juuuuuust right."

He laughed again, more nervous this time. "Should we . . . ?"

I stood up. "Yes, we should."

When we got in the car, he smiled and leaned into the middle and crooked his finger in a come-here motion. I laughed as I leaned over and he kissed me. "Where to?"

I didn't want to risk running into Kell, or anyone, right now. I'd been waiting an eternity for this. I wasn't risking any interruption. "Your place. No interruption, no flatmate —who I adore, mind you, but I want you all to myself tonight. Kell probably wants the place to herself tonight anyway—"

He silenced me with another kiss. "Don't be nervous."

"I'm not," I lied. "I'm totally calm and not nervous at all. Or worried that you'll regret waiting because, oh my God, he wasn't worth all that unresolved sexual tension, and you'd be really disappointed and have to take back that incredible tummy-butterfly comment. Which I'm never forgetting, mind you. It was probably the sweetest thing someone's ever said to me, so you can't take it back. It's mine now. I'm considering getting it tattooed on my body."

Merrick burst out laughing. "Tattooed? Like a picture, or the words?"

"Neither. I hate needles. I'm a total wuss, and I would absolutely, no doubt about it, puke or pass out. I'll honestly just have to keep having it redone in Sharpie."

He leaned his head on the headrest and stared at me, smiling fondly. "I would never take those words back. And I won't be disappointed, I can assure you. You are worth the wait, Leo."

I swallowed hard. "Have you considered asking Hallmark for a job? I don't know if they're hiring, but you could totally work there."

He laughed and started the car, then held my hand on my thigh the whole way back to his place.

I WAS NERVOUS. I couldn't deny it or pretend otherwise. But thankfully Merrick seemed to know without me saying it outright. As he reset the alarm, I wandered over to the shelves of various ceramic pieces that were for sale in the café. The overhead security lights lit up the room and I could see well enough. Of course, I'd seen the items for sale before, but I'd never really paid close attention. Now seemed like the right time, the perfect time to ask. It was the perfect distraction.

There were bowls, plates, platters, vases, cups and teapots, but there were also figurines of foxes and owls and ducks and tall statues and, wait, was that . . . "Is that your lamp? On your bedside table?"

Merrick was suddenly beside me. "Similar to, yes. Minus the lampshade."

"You made your own lamps?"

He chuckled. "I made nearly everything I own. Lamps, my wall clock, my entire dining set, coffee mugs, serving platters, soap dispensers. Somethings I need mechanical parts for, like the clock and soap dispensers, but yeah. I make it all."

"Wow." I couldn't believe it. These things on the shelves in front of me were high-end, quality pieces. "Which are your favourites?"

"To make? Or finished product?"

"Both. Either."

"I love throwing," he replied quietly. "Being at the wheel, that's what I love the most. But sometimes I love hand-building, too, and trying new things. But I love the firing process as well. What it does, and what different firing techniques do to clay and glazes is amazing." He went to one particular piece and picked it up. It was a large bowl that was a muted grey on the outside. It looked like concrete. But the inside of the bowl was a brilliant glossy purple that looked like a galaxy. "This has a triple process. Different firing, different glazes and oxides, at different temps."

It was breathtaking. "Merrick, it's beautiful."

His smile was serene. "Thank you."

"You really love what you do," I noted, stating the obvious.

"I really do."

"It shows in your work," I said. I picked up a cup. It was half white, half black, like it had been dipped in rough blackboard paint. "I don't know much about ceramics, or about art at all. But there's something about your work that . . . I don't know. Is sympathetic the right word?" I asked, more to myself than him. "Each piece is sympathetic to the person. The way it feels in your hand . . ." I tested the weight of it, the texture of it. "There's a kindness. Which is probably a stupid thing to say."

When he didn't say anything, I looked up at him to find him staring at me, his lips parted. "Leo, that was a perfect thing to say. Thank you. That's one of the best compliments I think I've ever received."

"Oh. Well, you're welcome." I put the cup back and moved on to the animal figures. The red fox was amazing. He was sitting with his tail around to his feet, and he had a cracked glaze effect on his chest, his nose, and the tip of his tail. "You made this?"

"Yep. He's cute, isn't he?"

"Gorgeous."

"They sell well. I had a complete series of beehive honey pots and an entire squadron of ducks in gumboots, but they all sold out."

"I should think so," I said. "Because who wouldn't want a duck in gumboots?"

He grinned. "I should make some more. They were fun."

"What's your most favourite thing you've ever made?"

"I had a woman who commissioned me to make the tiles for her kitchen splashback. That was pretty cool."

"You made kitchen tiles?"

He laughed. "Yep. She wanted the Moroccan tile look in a gloss-white kitchen. The end result was amazing. And I like the fact that my work is now a part of someone's house. That's kind of crazy."

"That's incredible."

"But I do go through different phases with different techniques. I love to try new things, like I said, but I also love the traditional stuff. Particularly the traditional Japanese and Chinese techniques. They're beautiful."

"Incredible like my little pinch pot?" I joked.

He laughed. "They don't even compare." Then his eyes lit up. "I have an idea. But you can say no if you want."

"Because that doesn't sound ominous at all."

He took my hand and led me through to the workshop and flicked on the lights above the sinks along the back wall.

"You want me to wash up?" I joked.

"No. I want you to throw with me."

"What?"

"At the wheel. I want to throw pottery with you." He looked so damn excited, but he quickly read my confusion.

"The pottery scene from *Ghost*? I wanna remake that with you."

Holy shit! "For real?"

"Yeah. You seemed to like watching me do it the other day."

"It was pottery porn, not gonna lie. Porn hub should have a pottery making category."

He laughed again. "So you want to try it?"

I took out my phone. "Siri, play 'Unchained Melody' by the Righteous Brothers."

CHAPTER EIGHTEEN

MERRICK

LEO SAT at the wheel and I pulled my stool up behind him, as close as I could fit. I was fully pressed against him, my arms around his waist and my chin on his shoulder. "This okay?" I asked, kissing the back of his neck.

He laughed, throatily. "Uh, yeah." He wiggled his arse, feeling my hardening dick pressed up against him. "Very okay."

I'd sat a wedged lump of clay on the wheel. "Put your foot on the pedal," I whispered. "Nice and slow."

I'd only set the wheel to slow because this was never going to be about throwing clay. I cupped his hands in my own, and together we pushed down on the clay. "Lean forward," I whispered. "Put your weight over it and gently push it down."

He leaned forward, sticking his arse against my dick. And so help me, he rocked back and forth. When he sat up straight, I pushed my chest against his back and put my hands over his once more. "Now we need to bring it back up."

I slowly squeezed his hands around the base of the clay

and added some slip for lubrication, and the clay began to form upward into a phallic shape. Then I moved his hands gently, slowly, up and down the clay. It was slippery and warm and very, very erotic.

"Oh my God," he murmured.

I kissed the back of his neck and pressed my weight against his back, my dick against the top of his arse. It felt amazing.

"Push it back down," I whispered. "Then work it back up."

"Oh fuck."

"How does that feel?"

"Like sex," he answered. "Like if you don't actually fuck me tonight, I might die."

I chuckled and gently bit down on his neck. He let his hands fall away and he leaned his head back on my shoulder. I tried to keep hold of the clay, rocking into him in a steady motion. He let out a groan and let his foot slip off the pedal, bringing the wheel to a stop. Leo shot to his feet and turned, straddling me quickly, rocking on my straining erection as he claimed my mouth with his.

His hands, smeared with clay, found my hair, my face, and I wrapped my hands around his back and pulled him closer.

I needed more. I needed more friction, more skin, more pressure, more everything.

"Upstairs," he breathed. "Before I let you fuck me right here."

I laughed and tried to catch my breath, but he stood up and swung his leg over. I could see the definite bulge in his jeans before he began for the stairs. Leaving the mess of clay exactly as it was, I chased him up to my bedroom.

He stopped at the foot of the bed when he suddenly

seemed to notice how clay-covered his hands were. When he looked at me, he laughed. "Oh. You have some clay . . ." He waved his hand at my face and hair. "Everywhere."

I grinned. "I'm not sorry." I held up my hands. "But you're gonna want me to wash them before I get to work on your body." I went to my en suite and laughed when I saw my reflection. He was right. I had clay everywhere. My cheeks, my hair, my neck. Leo bit his lip at my reflection in the faint light, so I cupped his face with my clay-covered hands and kissed him, smearing his face and hair too. "Now we're even."

We did wash our hands, not entirely thoroughly, but close enough. I was too worked up, too keen for this to finally happen, to be worried about the state of my sheets. They were gonna need washing anyway.

I towelled off my hands quickly, then began to unbutton Leo's shirt. If our desire had tempered any, it soon ratcheted back up as I kissed his neck, his chest.

He pushed me back against the bathroom vanity, his tongue in my mouth, his hands pawing at my jeans and my shirt like a man possessed. He wanted this so much, and I had every intention of making it worth it.

I got his jeans undone and he took a step back to pull them down. I took care of my own, kicking out of my shoes and pulling my shirt over my head. When we were both naked, I took a moment to take in his body. His lean body, the long lines of muscles in his thighs, his pale skin, and his rock-hard cock jutting proudly toward me.

He was glorious, and he was mine.

With my hands on his chest, I urged him toward my bed, the backs of his legs against the mattress. I pressed up against him, our cocks sandwiched and straining. I gently traced his jaw and ghosted a kiss. "I want you on your back so I can see it in your eyes when you come, when I'm buried inside you."

His nostrils flared and his cock jerked between us. "Fuck," he breathed, almost panting.

"Lie down, Leo."

He scampered up the bed, leaning back on his elbows. His legs were spread and his cock now lay against his hip. I took the new lube I'd brought and a condom from the bedside table and tore into it before I slicked up my fingers. He watched with dark eyes and heavy eyelids as I rolled it down my cock, and when I was done, he fell back against the mattress with a sigh. "God, I don't think I'll survive this."

I chuckled as I knelt on the bed, in between his legs. I kissed up his thighs, and ignoring his cock, I kissed, licked, and nipped up his belly. I sucked on his nipples, flicking them with my tongue, then kissed up his neck to his ear. "You're so fucking hot right now," I whispered gruffly in his ear.

He raised his hips and groaned impatiently. He really had waited long enough. I knelt back and pulled his legs over my thighs, making him gasp. Then I took the lube and slicked my fingers and his arse.

"Oh God," he whispered.

I pushed one finger against his entrance and slipped it inside him. And, like my art, I knew the way to get clay the most malleable, the most pliant and beautiful, was to coax it gently. Using enough restrained force and having it turn in your hand to produce the most amazing thing. It was about touch. And patience. And listening.

By the time I had Leo ready for me, he was moaning and writhing and leaking precome. With my fingers still inside him, I licked and sucked on the head of his cock, making him hiss and shake his head. And I knew then he'd had enough.

I lubed up my cock and leant over him, bringing his knees up. I positioned my cock at his hole and stared into his eyes as I pushed inside him.

He gasped. His mouth opened and his eyes went wide. "Merrick," he whimpered.

"I've got you," I rasped out before kissing him, pushing deeper inside him. He groaned into my mouth as I sunk all the way into him. He felt so good, so tight, and so hot. And he wrapped his arms around me and we started to move. Gentle rocking, slow thrusting, deep and consuming. He kissed me like he'd die if he didn't, and it was almost sensory overload; his tongue in my mouth, my cock in his arse, his fingers digging into my back, into my arse, urging me to go deeper, harder.

Leo began to roll his hips, and his groan got lower, his kiss more desperate. Oh God, he was going to come . . .

I pulled back so I could take his erection in my fist, and he gasped and arched. I pistoned into him and pumped his shaft, then he let out a strangled cry and his whole body went stiff. His cock spilled onto his belly and he convulsed with the pleasure of his orgasm, milking my cock inside him.

I leant over him and drove into him, hard and deep, and he gasped as I pulsed and filled the condom. He cupped my face and held me as my orgasm tore through me, a look of wonder in his eyes. Never had sex felt like this. Never had it meant this much. Never had I connected with anyone else like I did with Leo.

I collapsed on top of him, though he drew me in for a long, languid kiss. We were slick with sweat, come, and clay, but I didn't care one bit. I pulled out of him, then scooped him up in my arms, kissing and tracing soothing patterns on his back.

And I knew then, lying there with him like that, that I'd made the right decision in waiting. I needed to be sure, my heart needed to be sure, and it most definitely was. I'd never been surer of anything.

I kissed his forehead, his cheekbones, his lips. "That was amazing, Leo," I murmured.

He held me tighter. "It was." He pulled back so he could look into my eyes. "It was different and special. And really intense."

"I'm falling in love with you, Leo," I blurted out, surprising us both. His eyes went wide and I froze. "I didn't mean to say that. I mean, not like that. I didn't mean to say it like that—"

He kissed me hard, and I swear I could feel our hearts beating as one. He kept hold of my face but broke apart, gasping for air, with his eyes closed. "I feel it too," he whispered. "I thought I was crazy. It was too much, too soon, but it felt so right." He opened his eyes then, and I saw only truth in them. "I'm falling in love with you too, Merrick. You're amazing and smart and funny and talented." He sighed, a disbelieving sound. "I don't know what I did to make you look twice at me."

I pulled him so close and kissed him again. "You walked into my studio in your floral shirt, and you laughed at something Clyde said. I knew right then that you were different. That things with you would be different. Does that sound crazy?"

He laughed and put his hand to my cheek. "Not to me."

"Tonight's been amazing. I should probably go downstairs and clean up that clay. If it dries . . ."

He looked at the top of my head. "You have clay in your hair."

"I'll need to wash it too."

"We could shower together," he suggested with a smile. "Let's clean up downstairs together, then shower together. Then climb back into bed, and wake up together."

"I wish we didn't have to work tomorrow," I mused. "We could stay in bed all day."

"Me too."

"I could stay at your place tomorrow night, after work," I suggested. "If that's okay with you?"

"That sounds perfect."

I sighed happily. "I'm a bit scared now that we've crossed this bridge, we won't ever want to stop."

He chuckled. "I think you're right. I believe there's a lot more dicking to be done."

"More dicking?"

"Yep," he said with a laugh, but then he squirmed against me. "Do you think after we've cleaned up downstairs and showered, there might be some more dicking tonight?"

I kissed him with smiling lips. "If it's more dicking you want, then it's more dicking you shall get."

Leo laughed, but eventually his smile turned serious. "I meant what I said. It wasn't a knee-jerk reaction to you saying it to me first. I am falling in love with you. Maybe I'm already in love with you. You're an amazing man, Merrick. I still can't believe I got this lucky."

I took his hand and kissed his palm. "Ditto."

He gasped. "Did you just Patrick-Swayze-from-*Ghost* me?"

I laughed. "Twice tonight. Once at my pottery wheel and again just now."

"Well, let's get the mess downstairs cleaned up, then you can Patrick-Swayze me three times tonight."

I gave him a smiley kiss. "'I love you, Molly. I've always loved you.'"

He chuckled, a deep throaty sound. "That doesn't count as the third time." He bit his lip. "Well, maybe it does, just a little bit."

I laughed and rolled out of bed. I threw the condom into the waste bin in the bathroom and pulled on my briefs. Leo did the same, and I couldn't help but smile at our reflections in the mirror. I was covered in clay, he was covered in clay and lube, both of us had his dried come on our bellies—we were an absolute mess—but I'd never looked happier. He was just about beaming, his hair all messed up and his lips a little swollen, and I'd never seen a more beautiful sight.

"What?" he asked, looking at himself self-consciously.

I shook my head, and my heart was doing some squeezy-stumbling dance in my chest. "You. Just you." I kissed him softly. "Maybe I'm already in love with you, too."

FRIDAY MORNING'S pottery class was the last for this session from the Arcus Centre, and I was sad to see it end. I'd really enjoyed meeting this group of folks and wished I could get to know the class more. I'd spoken to the centre, gladly offering more sessions for their Bridge-the-Gap program because it was such a success.

As much as I was dreading it being over, I was also excited for everyone to try their hands at throwing on the wheel and for them to see their finished bowls. They'd all been taken out of the kiln the day before and it was always a thrill for me to see the reactions on faces as they saw the finished product.

Everyone had arrived, except my favourite three people. I knew they'd be the last in; Leo was picking Clyde and Uncle Donny up on his way, and as Shirley would say, Clyde and Leo usually arrived last.

I saw the front door open and heard Leo say hello to Ciara as he held the door for the other two. Uncle Donny came in next, and Clyde followed. Leo was grinning behind them. It wasn't really a smile for me, because Uncle Donny was wearing a pretty Japanese-style shirt with a long skirt. It looked as though it could have been traditional-wear, so it was unlikely anyone would question it.

But he was wearing a skirt in public.

My heart swelled with so much pride and joy, I thought it might burst. I went to the table and pulled out a seat, and my uncle gave me a small, proud smile as he sat down. Even Clyde smiled as he pulled his seat closer to Donny's, and Leo . . . well, Leo looked like he was made of sunshine.

Only when I could drag my eyes off Leo, I noticed Shirley. She was smiling so fondly at Clyde and Donny that I just about melted. "Nice of you to show up," she said, and when Clyde shot her a look, she grinned at him, giving him a wink.

He gave a nod in return. "Didn't want you to miss me."

Everyone waited for a sarcastic barb to follow that, but none came. It was possibly their most amicable exchange yet.

"Morning, everyone!" I said. "Last day today, which is a bit sad. First, though, we get to see our finished bowls, and then we can all have a turn on the potter's wheel. And to finish, I thought we'd wrap up the class today with some cupcakes I brought in. Because cake makes everything better. Even goodbyes."

"I already signed up for the next one," Joan said.

"Me too!" Shirley added, then looked directly at Clyde. "Sorry to disappoint you, Clyde. No 'accidental' drowning in the aqua aerobics next time."

Clyde sighed. "Then I suppose I'll have to come back here too," he said. Then he turned to me. "Someone has to keep Shirley in line, and there is no way Leo would let me go anywhere else anyway."

I grinned. "I'm very glad to hear that."

"Can we still have the cupcakes?" Harvey asked.

I laughed. "Absolutely." I clapped my hands. "Okay, we better get started or we will run out of time for cupcakes. Who wants to see the bowls we made last week?"

I lifted the cover on the table to reveal all the bowls. Everyone was so excited to find theirs, and Leo carried his, Clyde's, and Uncle Donny's back to the table. Uncle Donny's was perfect, and Clyde's wasn't far behind, but Leo's was . . . well, it matched his pinch pot.

"Look at it!" He held it up proudly to show everyone to a round of polite nods and smiles, but he wasn't deterred. "Look at how pretty it is!"

I laughed at him. "It's brilliant, Leo."

Clyde looked at me, then at the bowl, then back to me. He took off his glasses and held them out to me. Leo gasped, duly offended. "He's not blind," he cried.

"He obviously don't see too good, either," Clyde replied flatly.

"Are you trying to say something about me?" Leo asked, smiling.

"You, no. The bowl, yes."

Leo hugged his bowl. "Beauty is in the eye of the beholder."

Shirley joined in. "You'd think Clyde would know that."

"Is that how you chose that particular shirt, Shirl? Or were they giving them away at Gaudy dot com?" Clyde quipped back at her.

While they exchanged bickering barbs across the table, I pulled out a seat next to Uncle Donny. It was then I noticed he was wearing the purple bracelet today. Leo and I had bought him a purple one for his more feminine days and a green one for his masc days. "You look great," I said quietly. "I'm proud of you."

He gave a nod, but there was a smile that pulled at his lips. "I wondered if you and Leo would be free one day this week to take me to the Arcus Centre? To perhaps speak to someone about . . . what we talked about. Or next week is fine. I know you're busy."

I squeezed his hand. "I'd love to. What about Tuesday? Leo has Tuesdays off. He'll know who to speak to."

He gave another nod. "I'm still not sure what any of it means, but it's about time I figured it out."

"Perfect. And I know I offered before, but if you ever want me to take you shopping, in-store or even if it's just online, you only have to say the word."

"I know, and thank you. I think I'd like that." His eyes met mine then, and there was happiness there now, which I'd only learned had been missing in all the years I'd known him. He leaned in and whispered, "I think Clyde would like that too."

I chuckled and gave him a little nudge. "You just let me know when you want to do it."

Everyone was talking quietly about their bowls,

comparing and pointing out different things, but really, they were just being polite. Clyde, not so much. "Merrick, son, you busy?"

I stood up. "Okay, who's ready to get their hands dirty at the pottery wheel?"

"Leo is," Clyde replied. "Though I do believe it wouldn't be his first time."

I looked at Leo, who was staring at Clyde. He whacked his arm. "What the hell, Clyde?" He shot me a panicked look. "I didn't tell him . . . everything." His cheeks flushed pink. "God, Clyde. I told you that in private."

Clyde just grinned and held up three fingers. "I heard there was ghosting three times." His heavy brows lowered and he turned to Leo. "I thought you said ghosting was bad. Isn't that some young person speak—"

"Clyde!" Leo spoke over him. He was bright red by now.

I burst out laughing. "Leo!"

Uncle Donny clearly cottoned onto the ghost reference, and he gasped. "Merrick!"

"Shirley!" Shirley cried, raising her hand and looking at each of us in turn. "Would love to know what's going on."

Clyde pointed at Leo, then at me. "These two are boyfriends now."

Leo buried his face in his hands. "This is not how today was supposed to go."

"You are?" Shirley asked, very excited, her hands to her mouth. "How romantic!"

I laughed some more. *Boyfriends* . . . That term hadn't been used yet, but I certainly didn't object. I waited until Leo finally met my gaze. "Yes, we are . . . boyfriends?"

Leo's grin was instantaneous, and he nodded. Clyde

nudged him with his elbow. "See how easy that was? Told ya."

I laughed again, because this was all too bizarre. "Anyway," I said, taking control of the class again. "Let's try this pottery thing, shall we?"

There were only six wheels, so Leo, Clyde, Uncle Donny, and Shirley all waited while everyone else had a turn. I had to help and instruct, of course. I gave them each a small portion of clay and showed them how to use a little slip, and they each had a fabulous time. But every so often, I would hear a burst of laughter from someone, and when I'd look over, the four of them looked so happy. Each of them smiling and chatting away, laughing, and even Uncle Donny was laughing and talking . . . and so help me, I really liked these people.

They were good, *good* people. And I cherished the day they decided to walk into my studio. And knowing most of them were coming back for another series of lessons just warmed me right through.

When the first lot were done, it was Leo, Uncle Donny, Clyde, and Shirley's turns. Uncle Donny certainly didn't need any help, and Clyde was finally not great at something, clearly better at hand-building than throwing. Shirley squealed and laughed as the clay slid between her fingers, and Leo tried . . . and he'd remembered the basics, but in the end, when he realised it wasn't going to plan, he decided to make rude wanking motions up and down the clay instead until he squashed it with his hand.

"Okay, boss, you show us how it's done," Leo said, motioning to me and a wheel.

I sat and threw a handful of clay onto the wheel-head. I added a little slip and quickly had it centred before bringing it into a wide-based bowl shape. In just a few minutes, I'd worked the edges up to about a six-centimetre height. It wasn't perfect, but—to put it bluntly—I was showing off. I wired the bowl off the wheel to a small round of applause. "Wait," I said. I gently coerced the bottom edge of the bowl outward, then with slip on my fingertips, I bent the top edges into shape, pulling, smoothing, shaping until the round bowl was now a heart-shaped bowl. I held it out to Leo. "For you."

Everyone clapped and there were a few *awwww*s and Leo got a little teary, his hand to his chest. "Really?"

"There is no one else I'd throw hearts for but you."

He took the bowl, very gently. His eyes were glassy. "It's beautiful. Merrick, you can throw hearts for me any time."

I stood up and, keeping my messy hands away from him, gave him a quick kiss. Right there in front of everyone.

"Okay, Leo, that's enough fornicating in public," Clyde barked, but he was smiling fondly at us. "It's cupcake time."

EPILOGUE

TWO YEARS LATER

Leo

MERRICK FIXED MY BOWTIE, then flattened down the lapel on my suit. "You look amazing."

I looked at him in his suit and tie. "You're rather dashing yourself."

He sighed happily and smiled when I kissed him. "I just can't believe this day is finally here."

"Me either."

"Are you ready?"

"As I'll ever be."

"Then let's do this." Merrick let out a nervous breath and took my hand. "People are already starting to arrive."

We left the small room at the side of the altar and walked out into the main part of the church, which was almost full. Merrick's family filled one side, and the Arcus folk filled the other. Kell was in the front row on our side, wearing a killer blue dress. Selena sat beside her, looking hot as hell in a pantsuit. Merrick's Mum and Dad sat on the other side, all dressed up and fancy, smiling and proud. His mum gave us a wave, and Merrick squeezed my hand as we took our place in front of the altar.

"Why are you so nervous?"

"I don't know," he answered with a laugh.

Then the door on the other side of the altar opened and the priest walked out, followed by an almost unrecognisable Clyde. Even though I'd been with him this morning when he got dressed, seeing him in a tuxedo was nothing short of a miracle.

A hush fell over the church, and I guessed everyone had the same reaction as me seeing Clyde all dressed up. Well, except for Shirley, who burst into happy tears. He rolled his eyes and shook his head, but she dabbed at her tears with a hankie. The truth was, Clyde and Shirley were the best of friends, and although they bickered non-stop, they—somewhat begrudgingly—adored each other. They reminded me a lot of Ouiser and Clairee from Steel Magnolias. Clyde was Ouiser, of course. But when Shirley had taken a tumble a year ago, Clyde refused to leave her side. It was just a dizzy spell from her blood pressure meds, but it had scared Clyde a great deal. Not enough for him to be nice to her, evidently, but she finally knew he actually cared.

"You two don't scrub up half bad," Clyde said easily, not nervous at all. He nodded to Merrick. "But you better get on your side, son. The show's about to start."

Merrick gave my hand another squeeze and slipped across to stand opposite us, just as the front doors opened.

Donny was an absolute vision in white. He wore a freaking Vera Wang pantsuit, but the jacket was fitted at the waist with a train at the back. He was sporting a fresh haircut and subtle lip gloss. He held a bouquet of rainbow roses, and he owned that aisle in five-inch heels.

He. Was. Stunning.

Clyde gasped quietly and his eyes got all misty. I rubbed his back and he gave me a proud, teary smile.

Yes, they were doing a traditional church wedding. And yes, it was a black-tie event. I asked Clyde why they wanted to go all out and his answer was simple. "Because we can. For a long time, there were laws that said we couldn't." And then he'd added, "And Donny always wanted a white wedding, so shut your complaining, son, and hire a suit. A best man gotta have a good suit."

"Best man?"

"You hard of hearing too?"

Then I'd cried and hugged him, and he threatened to fend me off with his walking stick. Donny had asked Merrick to be his best man as well.

It had taken a while, but Donny had realised that the term 'gender-fluid' best described how he identified. Mostly masculine, some days feminine. He was happy with male pronouns but enjoyed wearing feminine clothes. Once he learned there were no hard rules or boxes he had to tick and he could be whatever the hell he wanted to be, he was truly free. Not long after that, Merrick had sat with Donny while they explained everything to Merrick's mum, and everyone took it all in stride. And Donny had smiled ever since.

So here we all were, in a church, on a glorious Brisbane spring morning, bearing witness to Clyde and Donny's love.

And standing with Clyde as he and Donny were married was freaking amazing. Though I'm not gonna lie . . . I spent the entire ceremony smiling at Merrick as he stood beside his uncle.

And when Clyde and Donny were announced husbands, Merrick took my arm and we followed them down the aisle.

The reception was gorgeous, filled with twinkling lights

and flowers. It looked like a magical garden party. Donny had planned every last detail immaculately: the venue, the music, the food. Clyde had gladly handed over control of everything, except his one rule of no speeches. He wanted everyone to attend, have a great time, then leave. Which was, by everyone's account, the perfect wedding.

We danced, we ate, we drank, and we danced some more. Everyone looked gorgeous all dressed to the nines, and it was, without doubt, one of the best days of my life.

When the dance floor had cleared a little, Merrick and I were still slow-dancing. "Today has been perfect," I whispered.

"It has."

I nodded to where Clyde and Donny were sitting at the head table, talking and smiling at each other with hearts in their eyes. "They look so happy."

"It's beautiful, isn't it?"

"I never thought I'd get all sappy at a wedding, but I totally am."

Merrick rested his forehead to mine and closed his eyes. Our feet had stopped moving, but we still swayed a little to the music. "Do you think that will be us one day? In our seventies and still madly in love?"

"I have no doubt."

He smiled and opened his eyes. There was a fierceness in his gaze that stilled me. "I thank all the gods that I didn't have to wait until I was seventy to get to meet you."

"Same."

"We shouldn't wait," he said. "Uncle Donny keeps telling me not to waste a minute. That every second waiting is a second wasted."

"Clyde says the same thing."

"Marry me, Leo."

My brain tripped over my heart. "What?"

He licked his lips and swallowed hard. "Marry me. Let's not waste another minute. Move in with me, marry me. Be mine, forever."

My heart squeezed to the point of pain. Sure, we'd talked about living together. When Selena suggested moving in with Kell, Merrick and I had mentioned in passing how it would be a natural step for us. But marriage? Getting married? This beautiful man wanted to marry me? Oh my God, there was so much to think about. "Would we hyphenate our names? Would I be Leo Secombe-Bowman? Or Leo Bowman-Secombe? Or do I just take your name and be Leo Bowman? That has a nice ring to it, I think. What do you reckon?"

He was smiling at me. "Is that a yes?"

"That's the yessiest yes in the history of yesses."

He laughed and kissed me, which was a little awkward considering we were both grinning. He laughed again. "Holy shit, you said yes."

"I can't believe you asked me," I said, shaking my head with the incredulity of it. "I mean, I was going to spend the rest of my life with you anyway, but if you want to make it official . . ."

Merrick hugged me so tight and we began to slow dance again. Eventually, he shot a look over to the head table. "Should we go tell them?"

"Nah." I shook my head. "Let them have their day. We can tell them tomorrow."

He kissed me again, sighing happily. "I love you, Leo."

"I love you, too. Future husband."

He chuckled and rested his head on my shoulder. "I wonder if I can make ceramic wedding rings."

"You can make anything. Oooh, what about ceramic

wedding invites? Or commemorative plates, like the Queen has. That could be fun. But heart-shaped ones like the heart-bowl you made me, of course."

Merrick laughed and gave me another smiley kiss. "Just the bowl? I've made you a lot of heart-shaped things."

"But that was the first."

He sighed and put his forehead to mine. "I promise you, Leo. I'll throw you all the hearts you want. From now till forever."

THE END

ABOUT THE AUTHOR

N.R. Walker is an Australian author, who loves her genre of gay romance. She loves writing and spends far too much time doing it, but wouldn't have it any other way.

She is many things: a mother, a wife, a sister, a writer. She has pretty, pretty boys who live in her head, who don't let her sleep at night unless she gives them life with words.

She likes it when they do dirty, dirty things... but likes it even more when they fall in love.

She used to think having people in her head talking to her was weird, until one day she happened across other writers who told her it was normal.

She's been writing ever since...

ALSO BY N.R. WALKER

The Dichotomy of Angels

Titles in Audio:

Through These Eyes

Blindside

Finders Keepers

Galaxies and Oceans

Nova Praetorian

Upside Down

Tallowwood

Free Reads:

Sixty Five Hours

Learning to Feel

His Grandfather's Watch (And The Story of Billy and Hale)

The Twelfth of Never (Blind Faith 3.5)

Twelve Days of Christmas (Sixty Five Hours Christmas)

Best of Both Worlds

Translated Titles:

Fiducia Cieca (Italian translation of Blind Faith)

Attraverso Questi Occhi (Italian translation of Through These Eyes)

Preso alla Sprovvista (Italian translation of Blindside)

Il giorno del Mai (Italian translation of Blind Faith 3.5)

Cuore di Terra Rossa (Italian translation of Red Dirt Heart)

Cuore di Terra Rossa 2 (Italian translation of Red Dirt Heart 2)

Rote Erde (German translation of Red Dirt Heart)

Rote Erde 2 (German translation of Red Dirt Heart 2)

Vier Pfoten und ein bisschen Zufall (German translation of Finders Keepers)

Ein Kleines bisschen Versuchung (German translation of The Weight of It All)

Weil Leibe uns immer Bliebt (German translation of Switched)

Drei Herzen eine Leibe (German translation of Three's Company)

Sixty Five Hours (Thai translation)

Finders Keepers (Thai translation)

CPSIA information can be obtained
at www.ICGtesting.com
Printed in the USA
BVHW030812250320
575946BV00001B/25